I0632659

Petals in the Snow

Jill M. Bagurdes

www.ten16press.com - Waukesha, WI

Petals in the Snow
Copyrighted © 2019 Jill M. Bagurdes
ISBN 978-1-64538-015-3
Library of Congress Control Number: 2019939596
Second Edition

Petals in the Snow
by Jill M. Bagurdes

All Rights Reserved. Written permission must be secured from the publisher
to use or reproduce any part of this book, except for brief quotations in
critical reviews or articles.

For information, please contact:

www.ten16press.com
Waukesha, WI

Cover photo by Sara Zawicki
Cover design by Kelly Maddern

This book is a work of fiction. Names, characters, places and incidents are
the product of the author's imagination or are used fictitiously. Characters
in this book have no relation to anyone bearing the same name and are not
based on anyone known or unknown to the author. Any resemblance to
actual businesses or companies, events, locales, or persons, living or dead,
is coincidental.

This book is dedicated to the memory of my mother Janet.
Your spirit has guided me every step of the way.
Missing you today, tomorrow, and forever.

Acknowledgments

For my husband Nick, who turned my doubt into hope and walked through the many stages of grief by my side.

For my sons Jesse and Dominick, who not only inspired the boys in this novel but who inspire me to be a good mother each day.

For my dad Thomas, who lost his life partner and poured out his emotions directly into my writing.

For my three older brothers and their families for sticking together and keeping Mom's traditions and legacy alive. (A special thanks to my goddaughter Sara for the cover photo!)

For Trixie Girl, who came into my life the year my mom died and sat by my side until I finished this book.

To Shannon, Carolyn, Lauren, and the rest of TEN16 Press for believing in my story and helping me to believe in myself.

To the rest of my family and friends who unknowingly helped me in my journey to write this novel, I thank you.

Prologue

It was day four of our hospice stay, and my mother was nearing the end of her life. The first day she was pretty aware and even commented on how beautiful the facility was. She also made a motion with her hands indicating she was worried about how expensive it might be. The second day she was starting to get confused, asking me what was happening to her. She turned to me and said, "Something's wrong, isn't it?" *Oh, yes, Mom. Something was wrong.* The third day she did not articulate very much, but she was able to reach out and give me a hug. A hug good-bye. The priest had already been here to give her The Last Rites. On the fourth day she had no response to us at all. The warmth had already left her body and she just lay there, mouth open, breathing very noisily.

I had spent the entire four days there including nights, only leaving to run home and shower and check on my family. I was convinced she would die the moment I left her side. I slept (sort of) on the couch in the room, waking every time a nurse came in to check on her. I had gotten to know the nurses pretty well, one in particular named Nicole, who had taken our family under her wing. She was in the room with me during those final moments. I found it both strange and comforting that a person I had met four days before was there with me as the life went out of my mother's body.

My dad and brothers had spent that last day there too but had already gone home for the night. We were trying to keep my dad in a routine so there would be at least some structure in these uncharted

1

waters. It was around 9:00 that fourth night when Nicole came into the room to check on Mom. I was constantly asking her how much longer, both needing and dreading her answers at the same time. She told me Mom's pulses were strong so she thought maybe a few more days.

We sat together on the couch with a blanket pulled over our laps. I asked her how and why she got into hospice nursing. It seemed like such a difficult choice for a profession. She told me it was an honor to be with people at the end of their life. I talked to her about my family, my teaching career, and, of course, the things that made my mom . . . my mom. We talked for about an hour, and I went over to the bed to look at Mom.

She looked different. Nicole came over and checked her pulse. She took out her stethoscope and then looked at me. She didn't have to say anything. I knew my brothers and my dad would not make it back in time, so I didn't even bother to call them. I sat by Mom's side and took her hand. This was really it. All the months of worry, tests, and treatments were about to be over. It was an unfair blessing.

I hugged her to me and told her over and over how much I was going to miss her. I laid her back on the pillow, and that was it. She was gone. Gone from this life and entering a new one. I was positive she waited for my dad to leave so that he would not have to deal with her actually passing. I don't think he could have handled it, my brothers either. I knew I was supposed to be the strong one, but all I wanted to do was crawl in that bed with my childhood blanket and lie with her.

Nothing would ever again be the same in my life without her. That thought terrified me. I had, God-willing, maybe forty years ahead of me, and she wouldn't be there. I would have to go through the rest of my life without talking to my mom. The nurse left the room to call my brother, giving me a few minutes alone with her. I stared at her lying in the bed, dressed in one of her nightgowns from home. The nurse had placed a rose on her chest and crossed her hands over it. I walked over to the front of the bed and put my cheek next to hers. I touched her soft hair that had not been cut in so long. "I love you, Mom. Don't forget about the rose petals," I whispered in her ear. I walked out of the room and went to the lobby area to wait for my dad.

Chapter 1

I heard the phone ringing as I entered the house, my arms loaded with bags as usual. I always told my husband Steve that any time I came home, he could assume I needed help carrying things in. It was my landline ringing. I must have been the only person left on the planet with a landline, but with two kids who weren't quite ready for cell phones, I felt like I still had to have one available in case of emergencies. I was guessing it was either a telemarketer or my dad, which were the only two who ever used the landline. I missed the call.

Oh well, I thought to myself. Whoever that was, most likely my dad, would call back. I set the bags down on the kitchen table and my little cairn terrier Trixie came running to greet me. She was the same breed and color as Toto from *The Wizard of Oz*. "Hi, Trixie!" I said excitedly and picked her up and snuggled her. I always greeted her like I'd been gone a year even if I had only been gone an hour. She was a rescue and was taken out of her home in Alabama. I felt the need to make that up to her constantly. "At least someone is here to greet me at the door," I said sarcastically and went to hunt for my family. I found my husband and kids in the basement playing some sort of video game.

Steve did not even look up from the screen as he said, "Oh, hi, honey, you're home."

I continued to stare at him until he finally glanced my way.

"Need any help?' he asked. My staring, which had now turned to glaring, forged on.

"I got it," I finally said, "as usual."

I headed back upstairs and began the mundane task of putting all the groceries away. My mind drifted to the week ahead as I planned out the dinners for the week. So Josh had track each night until five, Greyson had baseball practice on Tuesday and Thursday, and I had a spring sing to attend on Wednesday at the school I taught at.

"Steve?" I called down the steps.

"What?' he hollered back.

"What do you have in the week ahead?"

"Just practice with Greyson." Steve was the coach of the seven-year-old's team. So I began sorting the groceries by the nights ahead. It was like putting a puzzle together each week on who would be home at what time, who liked what, and what meals I could turn into two nights' worth.

I was also trying to decide what night to have my dad over. My mom had passed away about a year and a half earlier, and I was trying to help my dad cope as much as possible with his new life. It didn't really leave much time for my own grieving, but it sure kept me busy running two households. His childlike simplicity during the end stages of her death was somewhat of a blessing, since I really didn't have to deal with his emotional state at that time. He never really believed she was going to die, but now that she was gone, his naiveté was hard to deal with at times. He was still in the "I can't believe she is gone" phase, and it didn't look like that was leaving anytime soon.

I set out some lunch and called everyone up to eat. They came running like a stampede, including my husband. Sometimes, it was like I had three boys—just one was a lot taller.

"What are the plans for tonight?" I asked everyone.

"I thought I'd take the boys to see the new *Avengers* movie. Want to come?" Steve asked.

"Not even a little bit," I responded. "I actually need to get some work done, so I think I'll just stay back."

"Mom," Greyson said, "Work on a Saturday? You're a teacher!"

"Yep. Teachers work seven days a week . . . we just don't get paid for it." Steve rolled his eyes indicating he'd heard this before. We were nearing the end of the school year, but there was just as much work to do now as there was at the beginning of the year.

Josh, who was in sixth grade, asked, "Mom, can I get a phone? Everyone in my grade has one. School is going to be out soon, and how am I supposed to talk to people during the summer?"

I answered, "I don't know, Josh. By calling them on our home phone? Do we really have to have the conversation again about how I grew up without cell phones, iPads, iPods, texting, etcetera, and I still managed to hang out with friends? My best friends today are girls I went to grade school with. How did we stay friends for our whole lives without all this?"

"But Mom, things were different back then," Josh replied grumpily.

"We will let you know when we feel you are ready and responsible to have a phone." Josh mumbled under his breath and continued eating.

After lunch, I went to work outside in our yard a bit. It was early May, spring had finally sprung here in the Midwest, and things were finally starting to bloom. It had been a very cold winter, but thankfully not that much snow came. Winters sure seemed different today than when I was a kid. I remembered snow so deep we couldn't open our front door and having lots of days off of school. Now it just seemed to be a long, dark, cold winter, and I hadn't had a snow day from school in about five years. Teachers looked forward to them just as much as kids did.

I glanced around the yard deciding what to do first, but

unfortunately, I did not inherit my mother's green thumb. I still didn't even know what it meant to prune the roses. Steve did a lot of the outside work, but I sort of pretended to help by doing things like pulling out weeds and watering the flowers. We did have a nice area of rose bushes that I tried to keep in shape. My eyes welled up thinking of how my mom loved her rose bushes and took such precise care of them. I wished I had paid better attention when I was younger and she worked outside. Oh, well. Too late for questions now.

I moved away from the roses and went to work on gathering junk left over from winter. Steve decided to cut the grass, and the boys undoubtedly were back in the basement on their controllers. I really needed to get them out here now that the weather was getting warmer, but sometimes it's just not worth the battle.

Steve finished mowing the grass and walked over to me.

"I think I want to plant a new rose bush in my mom's memory," I said.

"That's a good idea . . . what color roses?" Steve asked.

"Well, we have a lot of pink and red right now . . . maybe something in yellow or white. I really wish I had paid attention to how she took care of them when I lived at home. You just don't think of those things when you are a teenager or in your 20s. You assume your parents will live forever and will always be here to answer your questions," I said in more of a bitter than sad voice. Steve looked at me sympathetically but didn't say anything. He never had to deal with something like this, so he just couldn't relate.

Married for about 15 years now, and things were perfectly fine but sometimes a little too much into a "friendship" phase. Both working full time, raising two boys, taking care of a house, my dad, and other obligations just didn't leave much time for date nights and romantic getaways like we had at the beginning of our relationship when all you can think about is getting naked with the other person. There was nothing quite like that feeling when you first start getting involved with someone. If only you could bottle that feeling and bring it out from time to time and pour it on each other.

I knew every marriage went through this phase, and talking with my friends I knew I was not the only one who felt this way. I just didn't want things to ever become complacent in my marriage. Sometimes it felt like I was waiting . . . waiting for something to happen. I didn't know what exactly.

We spent the rest of the day working outside and finishing up things inside the house. I called my dad to check on him as I usually did about this time of day.

"Hi, Dad," I said into the phone. I always called him on my landline because he never seemed to be able to hear me on my cell phone.

"Hi, Reagan, how are you?"

"I'm fine. Just calling to check on you. What are you doing?" I asked knowing full well how he was going to respond.

"Watchin' TV. There's a game on," he said.

"What did you do today?" I asked.

"Oh, not too much. I worked outside a little and ran to the store. What are you up to today?"

"I'm just about to make dinner, and then Steve is going to take the boys to the movies. Did you call earlier today?" I asked.

"No," was the answer I got.

"Oh. Okay. I'll probably stop over tomorrow if you need me to do anything at the house."

"Okay, honey. Thanks for calling."

"Okay, Dad. See you tomorrow." That was usually the extent of our conversations, but I really felt the need to call him every day to make sure he wasn't lying somewhere not able to get up.

I began chopping up things for a taco night. Greyson came running into the kitchen.

"What's for dinner? Oh, tacos! Yum!" he shouted excitedly. Taco night was a night that everyone liked and agreed on. "Can I help?" he asked.

"Sure," I said, and I gave him a few jobs to do. He loved to help me in the kitchen.

"Are you excited about going to the movie?" I asked him.

"Of course. Mom, can I buy popcorn *and* candy?" he asked as he carefully shredded some lettuce. I walked over to the cupboard and produced two movie theater boxes of candy, both of a sour gummy nature. His eyes widened with happiness. I refused to buy candy at the theater . . . it was such a rip off. Popcorn, yes. There was nothing like movie theater popcorn, but I usually snuck in sodas and candy. I did feel a little guilty, but by the time we got to our seats, I was usually over it. The trick, of course, was to open the soda when there was a loud noise or music coming out of the speakers. Otherwise everyone can hear the distinct snap and hiss of the soda can opening. Greyson helped me set the table, and we set out all the fixings for the tacos. He was such a helpful and sweet boy. Josh could be helpful and sweet too, but he was in a wonderful pre-teen phase that left him in various moods all throughout the day. We never knew which Josh we were going to get.

Everyone sat down to eat, and there was a lot of animated discussion about how this movie was going to compare to the previous ones. Never seeing the other movies, I didn't have a lot to add. I listened to their conversation and ate quietly. *I am lucky to have this family,* I thought to myself. Overall I was happy with the life I had created.

There was something about entering your forties that causes you to reflect on your life . . . the life you have already lived and the life that was to come. Maybe that's because it felt like a halfway point, since eighty seemed like the age to reach for. When someone died in their eighties, people generally felt like they had had a nice long life. If you went in your sixties, the comment would be that that was just far too young. If you're in your seventies, which was where my mom fell, it's sad but acceptable.

We finished dinner and they got ready to leave, pockets stuffed with candy and drinks. "Have a good time," I said, and they excitedly left the house.

After they left, I laid out my things to work on for the upcoming week. *This work would be a lot easier with a nice glass of wine,* I thought to myself. I poured a glass of Moscato into one of my mom's crystal wine glasses. Even though my dad was still well and living in the house we grew up in, I had started to take some items that I wanted. Nothing of major value but things that reminded me of her. My two older brothers could fight over my dad's stuff, but I was the only girl, so crystal and jewelry and photos were coming to me.

Although, unlike my father, I had accepted her death, there were many moments I still couldn't believe she was gone. At forty-two, I should have been picking her up for lunches and holiday craft fairs, not visiting her crypt at the cemetery. Fucking cancer. I sat down at the table and began to think about the week ahead. Trixie curled up at my feet and settled in for a snooze. I was soon immersed in reading and math lessons and began planning my daily curriculum outline.

My landline rang, and I glanced at the phone number that appeared on the TV screen, expecting to see my dad's number pop up. I didn't recognize the area code, much less the phone number, so I decided to let it go to the machine, and the caller hung up. I continued working on lesson plans and watching old episodes of *ER.* There was something about the opening music that just took me right back to my college days. I could remember waiting for

Thursday nights to see the continuing sagas of Dr. Green and the hot Croatian doctor. It's funny how the sound of the music of a TV drama can transport you back in time. The phone rang again with the same out-of-area phone number. Well, this person was certainly persistent, so I decided to pick up the phone.

"Hello?" I answered the phone with some annoyance in my voice.

"Hello," a male voice answered on the other end.

"Look. I'm on the no-call list, and whatever charity you're calling about I'm not interested." I especially hated the cancer charity calls—a lot of good "research" did for my mom. I knew it wasn't fair to think that way, but watching her die from two types of cancer had left me bitter. I was about to hang up when the voice on the other end said, "Is this Reagan Stills?" I paused. Stills was my maiden name.

"Who is this?" I asked.

"My name is Matthew Carlson. I'm calling from Florida in regard to my dad, Jonathan . . . Jonathan Carlson. You used to ummm . . . work with him." I think I literally stopped breathing. Then I hung up.

Chapter 2

I swallowed the last of my wine and sat on the couch staring at the TV as the doctors were running through the ER trying to avert some crisis. I was trying to remain calm, but that was hard to do when my mind was going about a million miles an hour. I knew who the caller was, but I had no idea why he would be calling me. I guessed hanging up on him was not the best way to figure that out. Just as I was deciding what to do, the phone rang again. The same number popped up, and I picked up the phone but didn't say anything.

"Please don't hang up until you hear what I have to say," Matthew said with a pleading tone in his voice.

"Okay. What can I do for you?" I asked in a surprisingly calm voice.

"I'm not calling to cause problems for you. My dad asked me to contact you," he responded.

"Why?" I asked with my heart pounding.

"My dad is very sick . . . he has cancer and the prognosis is not good. He's still in a good mental state, and I think he wants to get his affairs in order." I winced at the word affair. "He asked me, no, *begged* me, to get in touch with you. He wants to see you before . . . before . . ." His voice broke and trailed off. I wasn't sure how to respond, so I said nothing. "Reagan? Are you there?"

"Yes. What exactly do you know about me and your dad?" I asked.

"Enough to know that he wouldn't ask me to do this if it wasn't extremely important to him," he responded. Yes, it certainly was enough.

I closed my eyes for a second, and I was instantly transported back twenty years. An image of Jonathan and me running through the pouring rain filled my mind. This must be what it's like to have an out-of-body experience. All I needed was a little background music, and this could be a flashback scene from a dramatic movie. Sometimes I did that when I was driving somewhere and staring out at the road ahead. I would imagine different things that could happen, like winning the lottery or becoming a famous celebrity. I certainly had thought about this before . . . what it would be like to hear from Jonathan after all this time. But this wasn't a movie I was watching or a daydream I was having. This was real life, and it was actually happening, and I needed to figure out what to say, quickly.

"I'm not really sure what to say," I said in a cautious tone. "Where are you calling from, and where is your dad?"

"Well, I live in Colorado, but my dad retired to Florida a few years ago. He lives near Orlando with my mom. I took a leave from my job, and I'm staying with him right now to help him and my mom through this."

I paused and asked, "So, he's still married to your mom?"

"Yes." A slight wave of disappointment ran through me, but I wasn't sure why.

"Matthew, what happened between me and your dad was a very long time ago. I'm married, I have two sons. How would I possibly explain this? I don't even know how I could leave for a few days," I said.

"I realize this is coming out of the blue, but I'm just trying to take care of things for my dad. He's going to die and I'm powerless to stop it, but I'm going to do my best to fulfill his last requests. This was not something he spoke of lightly. He and I had a very serious conversation about this, and he was adamant that I get in touch with you," he said with sincerity in his voice.

"What did he say to you about our relationship?" I asked hesitantly. I suddenly remembered how Jonathan used to tell me that half of "our story" was mine and I could tell it any way I wanted to. I wondered how he had described his half of the story to his son. Matthew was younger than me by about five years, if I remembered correctly, which would put him in his mid-thirties. Jonathan was about twenty years older than me, which would put him over sixty at this point. It was strange to think of him as a sixty-year-old man, and I wondered what he looked like.

"He told me that he was involved with another woman a long time ago and that he wanted to see her one last time. He told me a little about what happened back then, but I'm quite certain I don't have the full story. He didn't offer an apology or any remorse and repeatedly emphasized how important this was to him."

"When did he tell you about me?" I asked curiously.

"About a month ago after his last diagnosis came back," he said and then sighed.

"Is that the first time he spoke to you about me?" I asked.

"Yes. I had no idea you existed until he sat me down and told me he had something to ask me." I stayed silent, thinking how life can change with one ring of the phone. I couldn't believe this was really happening. I thought for a few moments.

"Matthew, I appreciate your situation, and maybe if I was single, it might be something I would consider. I just don't see how I could explain this and take off from my family and head down to Florida. I'm very sorry about Jonathan. I lost my mom not that long ago to cancer, so I know what you are going through. I hope you understand," I said.

"If it's a matter of money, I can have a plane ticket and hotel all arranged for you," he said with desperation in his voice.

"Oh, it's not that. I can't do it, Matthew. I can't explain this to my husband. He would never understand this, and I just don't know how I could possibly make this happen."

Matthew was quiet for a very long time. "He's going to die, Reagan. I'm going to lose my father." He started to cry.

"I know, Matthew. Losing a parent is one of the hardest things to go through in life, and I'm sorry for what you are going through now and what you will be facing in the future." I had an immediate flashback of my mom's last moments, and I quickly shook my head, clearing those thoughts. It was so painful I couldn't think about it very often.

"Will you at least think about it for a few days and call me back?" Matthew asked. I said nothing. Over a million thoughts were circling in my brain. "I at least need to hear from you one more time. Even if it's just to tell me you can't come," he said. I experienced a sense of deja vu as I recalled a similar conversation I'd had with Jonathan at the beginning of our relationship. Our first "encounter" was at a bar, and Jonathan had expressed some feelings for me. In an instant, I was torn between my head and my heart. He told me that we at least needed to get together one more time outside of work, even if was for me to tell him I couldn't see him. "Reagan . . . are you there?"

"Yes. I'm still here. Matthew, I can't come. I'm sorry." There was an awkward silence that seemed to last for hours.

Finally Matthew said, "Okay, Reagan." And then as if he had one last card to play before the hand was over, he said, "He wanted to remind you about the rose petals." I did not respond. Then for the second time that night, I hung up on Matthew Carlson. He did not call back.

Chapter 3

"That was awesome!" Greyson shouted excitedly and burst into the house. I was sitting at the kitchen table, staring into a third glass of wine. I hadn't moved from that spot except to pour more wine since the phone call ended about an hour ago. Greyson's voice instantly brought me back to reality. He ran over to hug me and started to tell me all about the movie. I listened. But I was not really hearing his words. Then I started to get the guilty mom feeling, and I tried to listen better. "And then, Mom, there was this one part where . . ." However, I couldn't focus on anything he was saying.

"Wow, buddy. It sounds like the movie was pretty cool."

I turned to Josh, "Josh, what did you think of the movie?"

"It was good," was his very informative response.

Steve entered the house and said, "Hi, honey. Did you get a lot of work done?"

I thought of my empty lesson plan sheets but answered, "Yep. I'm all set for the upcoming week. Did you like the movie?"

"Yes. It was really good. The boys loved it," he stated.

"Okay, boys, time to get ready for bed," I said. Josh gave me his standard mumbling about how he was older and should get to stay up later than his little brother. I actually agreed, but from about nine o'clock until ten o'clock at night was the only time Steve and I actually had time alone together, since by ten I was usually passed out from exhaustion.

I got the boys down for the night and brought my glass of

wine down to our rec room, where Steve was already sprawled out watching some sports channel. I joined him on the couch and pulled a blanket over me. "This room is always cold," I said to him.

"Come. Let me warm you up," he said with that certain look in his eye.

I rolled my eyes at him and said, "I don't think so. This is the first chance I've had to relax all day." It was a familiar conversation between us.

"Uh . . . you had about two hours when I was gone at the movies with both our children," he said back at me. I sort of nodded, but I felt the expression change on my face thinking about the phone call I received. "I'm just kidding," said Steve.

"Oh, I know. Working on lesson plans is not exactly my idea of relaxing," I said with an irritated tone.

"Again, kidding," Steve said and then asked, "What's on the agenda for tomorrow?"

"I'm going to go by my dad for a while," I responded.

"Is he getting better do you think?"

"I don't know," I responded. "He still cries a lot and talks about how much he misses her. He just can't seem to deal with life without her. That's all he knows, life with my mom."

"Well, they were married for over 50 years, so how do you begin a new life after that long?"

"Right," I agreed.

Steve turned back to the TV, indicating that this part of our conversation was probably over. "Do you want some more wine?" he asked.

"Sure." He grabbed my glass and headed up to the kitchen. I heard him letting the dog out. I began having an internal debate about whether or not I should tell him about the phone call I'd received. It's not like I was going to fly off to Florida to do this crazy request, so I should just tell him. Steve knew about Jonathan but in a way you discuss all your past relationships. We talked about those things when we first started dating. He knew about my high school boyfriends and college flings, and he knew I was involved with someone older and married. He did not know, however, the extent and depth of our relationship. He just assumed it was just another college relationship that really didn't mean anything.

"Do you want me to find something else to watch?" he asked after returning to the basement.

"Sure," I answered, but we both knew it was only a matter of time before my eyes were going to close. It was really not a bad way to spend a Saturday night.

Steve grabbed the remote and flipped to *Saturday Night Live,* and we were soon cracking up over the political skits. The writers sure had a lot material, considering the state of our country right now. I was the least political person you would ever meet. I pretty much knew who the President was and that's about it. As a teacher, I should probably know a lot more about what's going on. Good thing I taught six-year-olds and government wasn't part of the social studies curriculum at that age. We continued watching the show, but my mind went to Jonathan and the earlier phone call. I'd thought about him plenty over the years for different reasons . . . a song that played on the radio from our time together, or if I drove by a particular place where we hung out. And, of course, any time I saw a pile of rose petals somewhere, I would think of him.

I started to think about how our relationship began. It began over nothing—a shared love of Pepsi. I was in college and working as a cashier at a local grocery store. Jonathan was the head manager of the store, and at first, I had very little contact with him. There were a lot of college kids working there, so I made many friends right away, and I hung out with them on our days off or after our shifts were over. I dated a few of the guys that worked there, but nothing serious. Jonathan was fine as bosses go, but I pretty much said hi and bye to him if he was working during any of my shifts. Then one day I was by myself in the break room, taking my scheduled 15-minute break, when he came in to get a soda out of the vending machine.

"Hey, Reagan," he said casually.

"Hi," I answered back. I was reading something for school and drinking a can of Pepsi. He pulled a soda can out of the bottom shelf, also a Pepsi, held it up, and said, "Cheers."

"My drug of choice," I toasted back. "I'm obsessed with it."

"Me too," he said.

He left the break room, and I finished my scheduled break and headed back to the front of the store. I continued my shift, but it slowed down, so I went to help work in the aisles. I was in the soda aisle stocking 24 packs of Pepsi cases when one suddenly broke open and the cans went everywhere, including a can that busted open and sprayed all over me. Jonathan turned the corner, walked over to the mess, and made some sort of sarcastic comment like, "Jesus, kid, you don't have to shower with the stuff. I get it—you're a Pepsi girl."

I cracked up at that, and we both knelt down and began picking up cans. I, of course, was a sticky, brown mess.

He said to me, "That's a great cola scent you're wearing, Reagan. You should wear it more often."

Then for some reason, I said, "Well, I'll have to spray myself with Pepsi more often now that I know it's your favorite."

I remembered that I flushed, realizing how that sounded now that it was out of my mouth. Our eyes connected then, and that was the first time I felt something stir inside me. He stared back into my eyes and laughed. We finished cleaning up, and then I got called back up front to help at the registers.

"Gotta go," I said standing up.

Jonathan handed me a can from the busted box and said, "Here, take one for the road." I grabbed the can and headed back up front. After my shift, I went downstairs to where the employees kept their personal items. I grabbed my purse and jacket out of the locker room and got ready to go home.

Jonathan saw me leaving and said, "Be careful of any Pepsi cans out there tonight. They can be very dangerous." I rolled my eyes and laughed. That night I couldn't get Jonathan Carlson out of my head. I remembered thinking that this was crazy. He was older and, for God's sakes, married! I wasn't sure where this feeling was coming from, but I knew I wanted it to go away, because it would lead nowhere. I cleared my head of thoughts of him.

I had the next few days off, but when I walked into the store on my next shift, there was a cold can of Pepsi waiting at my register. I looked around the front of the store until I spotted him. Our eyes met, I mouthed thank you, and he winked back at me.

All of a sudden, I realized that Steve was asking me something about the show. "What were you thinking about, Reagan? You looked a million miles away."

"Nothing," I replied, "I think the wine and the long week are just making me zone out."

"Do you want to watch a movie or something?" he asked.

"No. I'm pretty tired. I think I'm going to head upstairs to bed. Remember, I'll be heading by my dad's tomorrow," I said.

Usually I stumbled over to our unmade bed, crawled under the messy blankets, and fell asleep as soon as my head hit the pillow. Not tonight. Tonight I lay there thinking about my past and about a man that I fell so in love with that it almost scared me. I looked over at the cedar hope chest that sat in a corner of the room. I kept my most special possessions in there, including a white shirt that my mom wore so often her scent was woven into the fabric.

Whenever I felt the need to have her close to me, I took the shirt out, wrapped it around me like a blanket, and breathed deeply. It was both comforting and heartbreaking at the same time.

But tonight I didn't think about that shirt. I thought about a letter that was in an envelope that was at the very bottom of the chest. A letter that began *Dear Reagan, This is the hardest letter I will ever have to write.* I had not looked at or read that letter in a very long time. I knew that Steve would never go through this chest. Partly because he respected my privacy and partly because it just wouldn't interest him to go through something that contains old shirts, photos, and other mementos.

I was tempted to get out of bed and rifle through to the bottom of that chest and pull out the envelope that was simply marked Reagan with a line under my name. The first time I looked at that envelope sitting on top of my work locker, I remembered the mixed feeling of emotions that came over me: panic, sadness, heartache, and a small sense of relief. I remained in bed because I just didn't feel like stirring all those emotions up tonight.

I started thinking about what Jonathan must be going through at this moment. I knew too well the fear he must feel and the hope he had to reach for. I had not had the cancer diagnosis, but watching someone you love go through all the stages of this disease was a whole kind of hell in itself. It was sitting vigil every day, wondering if today was the day that the scan would light up or the disease would progress, or the last breath would be breathed. I wondered about his wife Karen and what she must be going through. I wondered how their marriage had been for the last 20 years and if she ever found out about the affair. It was a strange feeling knowing that if the other woman was ever discussed, it was me they were discussing.

I lay there tossing and turning. I couldn't go to Florida. It would be impossible. *Literally impossible,* I said to myself. I wouldn't be able to explain this request to Steve. He would think this was crazy, and he would be hurt. If the roles were reversed, would I be okay with him flying out to see some woman he had an affair with twenty years ago? Of course not. So that's it. Case closed. I told Matthew I couldn't do it, and I certainly didn't owe this to Jonathan. So I really didn't even need to think about this anymore. I eventually fell into an uneasy sleep, knowing that I would not be able to get this phone call out of my mind.

Chapter 4

I woke up early the next day before anyone else was up. Steve lay next to me, snoring quietly. I wondered what time he had stumbled up to bed. He always acted like he was irritated when I fell asleep early, but I knew he was secretly glad so he could play his PS4 as long as he wanted.

I stared at his chest rising and falling with each breath. He was a good husband and an even better father. I would never cheat on him or leave him under any circumstance. Was he my soul mate? I don't know, but he was a man I fell in love with and built a relationship and a family with. I wrapped my arm around him and snuggled up next to him. He stirred but did not wake up.

I lay there for a while and tried not to think about Jonathan, but it was near impossible. I traveled back down the memory lane road to the beginning of our relationship. After the Pepsi incident, we began talking more and more at work. I found myself hurrying to work just so I could see him a few minutes before my shift would start. Every time I took a break, he would happen to wander into the break room. Sometimes there were other people in there having their break too, and it would annoy me. But sometimes I was alone, and Jonathan would sit down at the table and we would talk for my entire break. I was often late going back on my shift, but I figured I was with the boss, so what could anyone do about it?

I certainly could feel something growing between us, but I would have tiny moments of doubt where I thought maybe it was just one-sided and he was just being a friendly boss. Then one day Jonathan stopped in the break room while I was busy reading some college textbook. He sat down, and we had some casual conversation. Then, as he got up to leave the room, he turned back and mentioned how a bunch of people from work were going to a bar on that Friday night, and he told me to stop by and have a Pepsi with him. I smiled and told him I would try, knowing in my heart I would be counting down the minutes to Friday night.

I heard Greyson's footsteps coming down the hall, and then he was by the side of my bed. "Hi, Mom. I'm up." *Well there goes my "me time" for the day*, I guessed as I looked at his sweet, little face.

"Good morning, sunshine," I said to him. I swung my legs over the side of the bed and followed him downstairs into the living room. I got him settled with a bowl of Cinnamon Toast Crunch and an episode of *SpongeBob* and then made myself a cup of coffee. Josh wouldn't be up for hours, and neither would Steve, so it was nice to have a little time with just me and Greyson. Well, sort of, since his eyes were glued to the TV, but at least we were hanging out together.

My phone rang, and I saw my dad's number pop up on the TV. He was calling to ask what time I would be heading over. After I hung up with him, I scrolled through all the calls in the memory. I decided it couldn't hurt to enter Matthew's number into my cell phone contacts. After I did that, I deleted the phone's entire call history. Ninety percent of those were my dad's calls anyway.

After a while, I went into the kitchen to make some food to take over by my dad. My mom did all the cooking and pretty much everything else around the house too. She was an excellent cook, and we all had our favorite things she made, mine being a special soup. It was one of the things I knew my dad missed the most about her, and I did too. She would still prepare special meals for all of us even into adulthood. There was always something so comforting about going over to their house simply because of the smells of the kitchen.

One of the worst moments I had after her death was on Thanksgiving Day. My mom still hosted all the holidays and refused to let any of us take over. As the holidays approached after her death, we all agreed to still celebrate Thanksgiving over by my dad, but we would obviously have to bring and prepare all the food.

I went over there early in the afternoon on that day and walked into a silent, empty kitchen. The table was not set with her fancy china, there were no pots boiling on the stove, and no holiday smells filled the air. I stood in the doorway and looked around, and my heart ached more than it had on the day of her funeral. Perhaps the reality was setting in, the finality of it all. There would be no more turkey dinners prepared by her. The holidays would be different now. I knelt down in front of the hutch that held her dishes and pulled out her blue printed china, plate by plate by plate. I was pretty sure a tear dripped on every single plate, platter, and bowl that day.

I sighed and began preparing some dishes to take by my dad: banana bread, pasta salad, a mini lasagna. I decided to make a small batch of her famous "kitchen sink" cookies. I stared at the recipe written in her neat handwriting. I looked at the list of ingredients, wondering if I had everything on hand to make it. Coconut, yes. Butterscotch chips, yes. Oats, yes. Yep. Okay. One batch of Mom's cookies, minus one mom, coming up. I knew my dad would never starve, but it made me feel better to bring him some things. By the time I finished making everything and cleaned up the kitchen, Josh woke up and came down the stairs.

"Mom, I have a project due at school tomorrow. Can you take me to the store to get some poster board?" Josh said, helping himself to some of the cookies cooling on the rack.

This was pretty typical of him to wait until the day before something was due.

"I'm heading by Grandpa's today, so Dad will have to take you."

"But Mom, I need it now. I have a whole project to do on it," he said in more of whining voice than I particularly cared for.

"Well, perhaps you should let me know more than a day in advance." I swore, sometimes teachers' kids were the worst kids when it came to schoolwork. He mumbled something and went to pour himself a bowl of cereal. That child was eating me out of house and home. As soon as that thought went through my mind, I laughed to myself. That was totally something my mom would have said. God, now I was using her expressions.

I threw on some sweats and a T-shirt, knowing I would probably spend part of my time over there cleaning. It was getting harder and harder running two households. My two older brothers were in the area, but one lived an hour west and one lived an hour east from my dad. Both had careers and families of their own, but they tried to help as much as possible. I lived the closest, so a lot of the responsibility fell on me. I packed up the food and grabbed my keys. I kissed Greyson and told the boys I'd see them in the afternoon sometime. I peeked my head in our bedroom doorway and saw that Steve was starting to wake up.

"I'm heading to my dad's," I reminded him.

"K. What time do you think you'll be back?" he mumbled, half-asleep.

"In the afternoon, well before dinner time," I responded. I headed out and began the 20-minute drive to my dad's house. I decided to take the side streets instead of the expressway. I blared my Ed Sheeran CD loudly and began singing "Castle on the Hill" at the top of lungs in my non-singing voice. I loved that song, and it totally made me think of my younger self and all the crazy shit I did with my friends.

I began thinking again of that first encounter with Jonathan. I did, of course, end up going to the bar on that Friday night. I drove there with the anticipation of a first date even though it wasn't. I couldn't recall the name of the bar, but I did remember pulling up and waiting in the car in the parking lot for a few minutes. *What was I doing?* I thought to myself. *This man was my boss, this man was married, this man was older* were the thoughts that went through my head. He was probably not even on the same wavelength as me. Numerous doubts went through my head, but I reapplied my lipstick and headed inside.

There were a bunch of people from work already there hanging out at the bar, and I quickly joined my friends and ordered a drink. I tried to casually look around for Jonathan and spotted him sitting at a table with a bunch of assistant managers, talking and laughing. He didn't look up to see me or come over by me. I remembered feeling very impatient with myself. This was not a date. This was a bunch of people from work going out on a Friday night, so I should be treating it as such.

I was there for about an hour or so when Jonathan came over to the bar and sat beside me.

"You made it," he said.

"Yep," I said.

"I'm assuming that is a Pepsi?" he asked me in a teasing voice.

"Mmmmm . . . with a little extra in it," I said. I had a passion for brandy and cokes, which I think is a Midwest thing, because whenever I have traveled, bartenders looked at me strangely when I ordered it.

I couldn't remember exactly what we talked about at that bar, but I just remember feeling this undeniable attraction, and I had no idea if he was feeling it too. I didn't hang out with just him the rest of the night, but I was constantly aware of his presence. People began leaving around midnight or so, but I stayed with a few of my friends. Jonathan also continued to stay, but he was talking to some people at the bar. When the last of my friends took off, I decided to leave as well.

I hadn't drunk anything in well over an hour, and I felt fine enough to drive home. I headed to the bathroom to pee before heading out. When I came out of the bathroom, Jonathan was in the back hall waiting for me. I walked toward him, and he grabbed me and pulled me toward him. My eyes locked onto his and I could barely breathe. He leaned down and placed his lips on mine, and we shared the most amazing kiss.

I realized I had just driven 20 minutes to my dad's house and I had no idea how I even got there. I pulled in the driveway and shut the car off. The garage was open, and his car was sitting inside it. It was still a surprise to just see one car. We had given my mom's car to one of my nephews shortly after she died. I gathered up the bags of food and headed inside. I walked into the kitchen, and while it was certainly not as painful as a holiday, it still made me catch my breath to not see her standing at the stove cooking or sitting at the table, going through some catalog and saying, "Hi, Reagan."

There was just silence. You just never realize how loud silence can be until you walk into the empty kitchen of your deceased mom.

"Dad?" I called out. "I'm here." I walked over to the fridge and began putting the things I made inside. I took a quick look at all the shelves to make sure there was nothing spoiled or outdated. He had a habit of buying things and then forgetting he bought them. I heard him shuffling down the hall from a back bedroom that he had turned into a TV room. I knew he spent a good portion of his day sitting in a recliner watching his shows. He was only a few years older than my mom, but he looked closer to eighty. He had really aged in the past year, especially in his eyes. Gone were the crinkly laugh lines around his eyes, and instead they were replaced by a deep sadness that seemed to come directly from his soul. *How did this happen?* I thought to myself for the millionth time. How did *my* mom die?

"Hi, Reagan," my dad said and gave me big hug like he did every time he saw me.

"Hi, Dad. How are you today?" I asked.

"Okay," he said with a small smile, trying to look like everything was okay.

"I brought some food over for you to eat. I put it in the fridge."

"Thanks, honey. How are the boys?"

"Good. Already counting down to the end of the school year. Memorial Day is only a few weeks away, and after that it's all downhill," I said.

"For you too," he laughed.

"Yes. I'm definitely ready for summer vacation! Are you planning on doing a garden this year?" My mom loved to garden. She planted all sorts of vegetables including tomatoes, green beans, cucumbers, and even pumpkins. My boys loved going over to their house in the fall and picking their very own pumpkins. I, of course, could barely keep our grass alive, so we didn't grow much in the way of veggies except for tomatoes. My mom also had a huge wildflower garden and then, of course, all her rose bushes. I wasn't sure what my dad was going to do with all of that now.

"I don't think so," he said sadly. "Your mother is really the one who did all that."

"I know, but maybe Steve, the boys, and I could all come over and plant a small garden for you."

"Maybe," he responded without a trace of enthusiasm.

"I know how hard this is for you, Dad, but Mom would want us to keep her traditions alive." His eyes began to tear up so I quickly changed the subject. "Well, I think I'm going to get some cleaning and wash done while I'm here."

I also did not inherit my mother's love of cleaning. My house generally looked like a tornado had gone through it. Not her house. It was always immaculate. I never understood how her mirrors looked so shiny and mine looked like they had just been smeared with toothpaste . . . and this was after I Windexed them. But I tried my best to keep her house looking the way it did when she was alive. I knew that would have been important to her.

"Okay, honey. I'm going to watch some more of the game." And with that he headed back to the TV room, and I could picture him settling in the recliner. I supposed the sounds of me bustling about the house cleaning were comforting sounds to him, a bit of his past returned.

So I set about with the routine that had become familiar to me in the last year. I went to their laundry room and sorted all my dad's clothes and began a load of his clothes. I always did that first so that I could at least get a couple of clothes washed and dried while I was there.

I stared at the shelf that contained all the various bottles of detergents. At my house, I have one bottle of Era and one bottle of Shout. My mom, of course, had something for every kind of stain, and a lot of the bottles still remained on the shelf. There was one bottle that just haunted me every time I went there. Fabric softener. I hated it. Why? Because I never had understood how, when, or why to use it. And now I couldn't ask her.

Next I did the two bathrooms. Surrounded by boys at home and now cleaning my dad's toilets, I cleaned up more pee off seats, floors, and even walls than I would care to admit. Every time I cleaned the shower, I pictured one of the last intimate moments I had with my mom. She had just come home from the hospital after being there for two weeks straight. She was in desperate need of a shower but couldn't do it by herself. I had to undress her, help her get in, and wash her entire body. The bath brush I used to scrub her back still hung in the corner of the shower. I touched the smooth wooden handle, remembering what it was like to bathe her. I thought she would feel strange, embarrassed even. She didn't. I didn't either, feel embarrassed. Part of me felt strong, that I was taking care of her. Part of me felt scared . . . that I was taking care of her.

The last room I always did was my mom and dad's bedroom. It still looked pretty much the same as the day the ambulance came to take her from her home and transport her to the hospice facility. I stared at her side of the bed and pictured her on the last day in this house. That morning I had fed her in her bed what I think was her last food ever. Homemade applesauce. I had made it that weekend while decorating my house for Halloween because, of course, I had to have the scents of fall fill my house while putting up my pumpkins and witches.

Watching her being wheeled out on the stretcher for the last time was one of the worst moments of my life. My dad, brothers, and I stood in the doorway of the house, numb from the pain, and watched them take her out the door for the last time. The ambulance drivers were nice and trying to comfort my dad. *What a shitty job*, I thought, *transporting people to their impending death*. They shook my dad's hand and told them how sorry they were.

Through his tears, he whispered, "Take good care of her."

One of them said, "Like she's my own mother."

How many times had they said that? How many times had they wheeled one half of a heart away from the other half? She had been pretty out of it for days by then, but as she was being wheeled out of the house, she kind of woke up, squinted at the house, and said, "I know I'm not coming back." I wanted to reassure her. I wanted to tell her that she would be okay, that she would be going to a better place. But the lump in my throat would not allow me to push any words past it, so I said nothing. I hoped she could see in my eyes what I wanted to say.

And that was it. They put her carefully into the back of the ambulance, and we watched as they drove down the street, taking her away from her life as she knew it, forty years in that house she had loved and cared for. I wished now I had gotten in the ambulance with her, but I had to drive my dad over to the hospice facility. He was in no condition to drive, not that I was much better, but I had to be strong for him. I barely remembered driving there, but we pulled into the circular drive of the hospice building just as she was being pulled out of the ambulance. We weren't able to see her right away, and I wondered what the hell was going through her mind. I knew what was going through mine: this was not really happening.

I shook my head clear of thoughts of hospice and glanced around their room. I had gotten rid of pretty much all her clothes right after she died, but that was about it. Her perfume bottles were still laid out in a semicircle on the dresser. Her jewelry box remained untouched, and her bookcase was filled with all of her favorite novels and knickknacks. Never one to get a Kindle, she preferred to actually turn the pages of a real book.

I ran my hands over her books and remembered all the conversations we'd had about different novels and authors. I grabbed a book that I had never read from the top shelf and sat down in front of the bookcase and read the back jacket. I always had intentions of reading all summer long, and I was lucky if I got through one novel. My mom was in the middle of a book I had bought her for her birthday when she died, a piece of paper marking the last page she read, page 256. There were still about thirty pages to go. I kept that book on my nightstand, and I'd thought about taking it to the cemetery, sitting down in front of her crypt and reading those last thirty pages to her. She didn't even get to finish the fucking book, much less see the movie they made it into.

Anger flooded through me, and I stood up quickly to put the

book I was holding back on the top shelf. When I did that, I bumped into the shelf, and a folded piece of paper fell onto the ground. I picked it up. It was my mom's distinct handwriting, and on the front of the paper, it said, *My Last Wishes*. Where the heck did this come from?

I was about to take a look at it when I heard my dad say, "Reagan, do you want some lunch?" I shoved the paper into the book I had been looking at and carried it in my hand into the kitchen.

"Sure, I'll make us some sandwiches," I said to my dad. He looked at the book I was holding in my hand, and I said, "I'm going to borrow this one and hopefully get through it this summer."

"Sure, Reagan. You really should go through all her books and take the ones you want," he said with a sad smile. It was so unbelievably painful to watch him try to live his life without her. I made us some turkey club sandwiches and set them on the table. I poured us some lemonade and also put out chips and pickles, trying to replicate the kind of lunch my mom would have prepared for him. It would never have been just a sandwich. For God's sakes, a meal wasn't a meal at their house unless there were four sides to go with it on the table as well.

We sat down to eat, and I knew my dad appreciated having someone to eat with. I felt that was one of the worst parts for him, sitting at the table and eating alone. Who would want to eat every meal alone and stare at the surrounding empty chairs? *Fuck, fuck, fuck cancer.*

We began to eat and had small chatter about the upcoming summer vacation. It was a great benefit about being a teacher. I would be home with the boys all summer and not have to worry about what to do with them.

"What are your plans for the summer?" my dad asked.

"Oh, the usual stuff," I replied. Of course, being a teacher, I loved the season of summer. The time off was well needed, and I looked forward to all the things we did as a family. Each summer we made a bucket list with everything we wanted to do. "The boys put swimming, fishing, lemonade stands, and drive-in movies at the top of our list this year," I said.

I also knew I would try to spend as much time with my dad as possible. We sat in silence for a few moments, and I had to fight the urge to read the note that I stuffed into my mom's paperback. I had no idea she had written something like that. I hadn't had a chance to open the note all the way, so for all I knew it was a blank piece of paper. One time I had given her a blank cookbook that was titled *Recipes from Mom's Kitchen*. In it, I had listed all the special dishes she'd made for our family over the years: Her famous potato salad, Christmas cheesecake, and oxtail soup, to name a few. I'd asked her several times to write her recipes down in this book for me.

I found the book recently while going through her cabinet of cookbooks and recipes. After thumbing through the pages, I discovered the entire thing was still blank. She had never written down a single recipe! I had a few theories on why that was. Maybe she forgot I gave her the book. Maybe she intended to do it "later." Maybe she wanted to take her recipes with her to the grave, as many of them came from her head and not necessarily from a piece of paper.

I hosted the first Easter after her death, and I tried to duplicate her hot spinach salad dressing without a recipe to go on. It was pretty much an epic fail, but everyone tried to pretend the thick, hot dressing that tasted like sweet cornstarch was "just like Mom's." I'd never know the reason she didn't write the recipes down for me, but I sure as hell wish she had. I could just add that to the list of wishes and regrets.

The end of my mom's death went very quick . . . too quick. I think that was a shock to us all. When her lung cancer spread to her kidney, we knew that it was not going to be long. When my mom called to tell me it had spread, all she said was "It's not good." She received the test results in September and was gone by mid-October. The timing of it was especially sucky for me because the school year had just gotten underway, and it was an incredibly busy time. Also, of course, she picked this time of the year to leave because even though summer was a teacher's best friend, I loved the season of fall and all that came with it. I especially loved decorating for Halloween and the smell of the fall night sky. Now that time of year would be forever changed for me.

No one was prepared for how fast she was going to go. She had a fucking chemo appointment scheduled for the week after her death. The oncologist, not wanting to give up, I suppose, never told us that it would be that quick. It took a visiting nurse who stopped by for a routine check to tell us that her oxygen levels were significantly low and that it would not be much longer. She was gone four days later. There was not a lot of time for conversation as her body began to shut down so quickly. She was a woman always in control, so to see her so incapacitated was a frightening experience.

The fast end to her time here on Earth was both a blessing and a curse. I wish I'd had more conversations with her about her life, what she meant to me as a mom, and what my life would be like after. However, we really didn't have that kind of relationship to begin with. We were close and probably spoke every day of our lives, but there were not a lot of "Hallmark" moments.

We finished eating, and I cleared the table and began putting things away in the fridge. After I was done, I said, "Well, Dad, I think I'm going to head home. Is there anything else you want me to do?"

"No, honey. You do so much for me. I don't know what I'd do without you," he said with great emotion in his voice. My dad and

I had always been close too, but the death of my mom had brought us much closer. I wanted him to know that I would always be here for him, and I wanted to make sure I had the types of conversations with him that I'd neglected to have with my mom, for he too would be gone someday. I gave him a hug good-bye, and he pulled me at arm's length, looked in my eyes, and said, "You are your mother's daughter."

I didn't respond, but once again it made me think that as much as he loved me, it was probably hard for him to see me sometimes. Being the only daughter, I could only remind him of what he had lost.

I gathered up my stuff, including the book I had pulled off the shelf earlier, said good-bye, and got in the car. I pulled out of the driveway and intended to start down the road that would take me on my scenic route home. Instead I turned the opposite way and headed for the cemetery.

Chapter 5

As I drove to my destination, my mind drifted away from my mom and toward that night at the bar, the night when Jonathan kissed me for the first time. When we pulled apart after that kiss, I didn't know what to say. I think I said something like, "So, this isn't just employer-employee anymore, is it?"

He said, "Definitely not."

I then said, "And this isn't just friends anymore, is it?"

He kind of looked down and smiled and said, "Not exactly."

"Well, what is it then?" I asked him kind of playfully. I remember feeling nervous but excited, because I knew my feelings were not one-sided.

"I don't know if that's up to me," he responded.

"Well, you're married, aren't you?" I asked, hoping for a response I wanted, like maybe they were in the middle of a divorce. All I got was a quiet "yes."

I gave him a look like, well, what the hell am I supposed to do with that piece of information? His words came out very carefully and sincerely. He told me he was very attracted to me and that he had developed feelings for me. He wanted to see me outside of work but understood if I couldn't or didn't want to get involved. He asked how I felt about him. *Well I think I'm pretty much falling for you,* I thought in my head, but, of course, I was not going to say that out loud. I didn't know what to think or say, but I sure as hell knew what I was feeling. I didn't want to feel it, but how do you control something like that?

"Would you be interested in seeing me outside of work?" he had asked.

"I'll have to think about it," seemed the safest answer at the time. The smartest answer? Of course not. The smart thing, the intelligent thing, the reasonable thing to do would have been to say, "Hey, dude, you're fucking married. That is a deal-breaker in anyone's eyes. I'm out."

But as I looked into those denim-blue eyes, I couldn't do it. This was not just a sexual attraction but an emotional attraction to this human being.

"How fast do you think?" he had asked with a sweet look in his eyes. He grabbed me by the waist and said, "I at least want to see you one more time away from work. Even if it's to tell me you don't want any part of this."

"Okay," I said. We said good night, and I walked out of the bar, got in my car, and drove home thinking my life would never be the same.

ℰ℘ ℰ℘ ℰ℘

I turned the car into the entrance of the Evergreen Cemetery and began the drive down the narrow, winding roads that would lead me to her crypt. She'd had pretty specific instructions about her funeral arrangements. She didn't want a wake, she wanted a closed casket at the funeral, and she wanted to be put into one of those wall crypts. She always said, "I don't want everyone looking at me." We held true to two of the three wishes. We kept her casket closed although, strangely, she looked better in her casket than she had on her deathbed.

I had been the one to pick out her clothes. I chose a top I especially liked on her and a pair of black pants. Her mother's ring, with mine and my brother's birthstones, was placed on her finger. Around her neck, she wore a necklace with little boy and girl shapes representing each of her grandchildren. She was buried in just those two pieces of jewelry. We also placed photographs and drawings from the youngest grandkids around her. Somehow it made me feel like we would be with her in that casket. About an hour after she died, I removed her wedding ring from her finger. Physical changes happen very quickly after death, and her body was already changing. The cold touch of her skin freaked me out, and I pulled off the ring as quickly as I could. Her ring was just a single, gold band, and I wore it around my neck every day.

My brothers and I had gone to the cemetery months before she died to purchase a joint crypt for our mom and dad. We did have a wake for her, but we called it a celebration of life so she wouldn't be angry. There were too many people in our lives to not have something where people could come and express their condolences. My dad especially needed it, and he held up surprisingly well throughout the three-hour ordeal.

He really only broke down when they played Elvis Presley's "Can't Help Falling in Love." How many times had they danced to that song over the past 53 years, including all of our weddings? My brothers and I sat close to my dad during that song, looking everywhere but at his face. He stood up toward the end of the song and moved next to the closed casket and placed his hand on top of it. His final dance with her.

It's morbidly weird how much a wake is like a wedding reception. Everyone's dressed up, you see people you haven't seen in forever, and everyone stands around having these insignificant conversations. The image of all the grandchildren dressed in these grown-up suits and dresses, laying roses on the casket, was burned in my mind forever. And there I was in the middle of it all, wanting to scream, "Hey, that's my mom's dead body in that box, you know."

I parked my car on the side of the road near the path that led to her crypt. I grabbed the book from my bag and walked slowly up the path, nodding to a few people who were paying their respects to their loved ones. Every time I came here, I always hoped that there would be no one else in that area so I could talk or cry in private. I turned the corner and didn't realize I was holding my breath until I felt myself exhale when I saw the empty sidewalk in front of the wall that held her crypt. I walked toward it and stood in front of her name. Ann L. Stills, 1944-2016, was engraved on the crypt. I stared at the wall that held my mother's body, and I had to remind myself again that *she* was not in there. I pictured the first few times I had visited the cemetery with my dad after her death. Watching him talk to the metal plate and asking out loud if she could hear him nearly broke me in two. It took him so long to come to the realization that my mother was not actually coming home again.

Next to it was my dad's name, Michael L. Stills, with his year of birth, 1942. There was no date of death listed yet, of course. My mom never got a chance to see her final resting place, but my dad obviously got to see his as he visited her probably twice a week. A simple crucifix was engraved above both their names. I stood in front of the crypt for a long time, thinking again for the millionth time that I couldn't believe I was standing in front of my mom's crypt and there was a date of death stamped on it.

I sighed and sat down on the bench in front of the wall and set the book next to me. My phone began buzzing, and I glanced at the screen to see who was calling. Steve's number popped up, and I figured he was calling to see how much longer I would be. I didn't answer, and the phone stopped buzzing. *I'll call him back in a bit.* I glanced down at the book next to me and the little fold of paper that was sticking out of one of the pages. I grabbed the paper and slowly pulled it out of the book. Did I want to read this? Would it make me sad or happy?

I unfolded the paper carefully and saw that there *were* words scrawled across the paper. Not blank. I smiled to myself, relieved. I still gasped at the sight of her familiar handwriting. *My Last Wishes* was written again in her careful script across the top of the paper. I began to read what might have been my mom's final thoughts. No date was listed, so I was not quite sure when she wrote this in her cancer journey.

My Last Wishes

These wishes are not for me, as I will soon be gone and my wishes are all used up. There is no lamp to rub and no genie to grant me any more. These wishes are for my husband Michael, my children Robert, Ryan, and Reagan, and my seven grandchildren.

For Michael, my death will be hard, nearly impossible for you. I wish you peace and strength as you journey through act three of your life without me. I had not planned to leave you so soon, but God had other plans for me. Do not worry. The kids will help take care of you. You are not alone. And I want you to remember this. You did not die. You still have life to live and children and grandchildren who need you. When the time comes, I will be waiting for you with open arms at Heaven's gates and we will once again be together. I love you with all my heart. Thank you for over fifty years of marriage, love, family, and faith.

For my sons, Robert and Ryan, I wish you many happy memories with your own families. I wish you courage in the hard times and gratitude in the good times. Be generous with your time and love. Please take care of your father.

For my grandchildren, I wish you success in all your schooling and luck in all your future endeavors. I am sorry that I did not get to see you all grow into adulthood, but I will watch over you for the rest of your lives. Choose a partner who will make you happy but will also challenge you to be the best person you can be. And know that at every graduation, wedding, and births of children I will be present.

And finally to my only daughter and last-born child Reagan, I wish you the ability to know how strong you are. I watched you learn and grow from the mistakes of your past. I watched you grow into a wonderful woman, wife, and mother to your two boys. I am proud to be your mother. Do not leave this world with any regrets. I love you and will miss you.

I stared at the paper, not quite believing I had found this. In the forty-two years I'd known my mother, I had never heard her speak like this or saw her write anything like this. She did not express a lot of emotion, though I always knew she loved me. My mother was a very strong woman. I never saw her worried, anxious, or stressed about anything, or at least she never showed it. If something needed to be done, she simply just took care of it. She faced problems head on, and I think she enjoyed the challenge of fixing things. I, on the other hand, worried constantly, especially as a child. However, I always knew she would take care of things for me. Sometimes, when I was very young, I used to cry myself to sleep at night, so afraid she might die. Even into my adult years, I worried about her death. What would I do? How would I survive?

On the night of her death, I was alone with her for a few moments in her hospice room. I stared at her body lying in the bed and said out loud, "Well, Mom, the very thing I was afraid of my entire life has just happened." However, I felt something inside me change after her death. I was, of course, profoundly sad and grieving her loss. But I didn't fall apart like I always thought I would. I had a funeral to plan, children to comfort, and my dad to take care of. I simply took care of things . . . just like she would have. She'd been gone a year and a half, and I missed her every second of every day, but I hadn't let her death take over my life. She would never have wanted that.

I picked up the paper and read her final words to me again, and it was as if I could hear her saying them out loud to me. I knew I had to share this with the rest of the family at some point, but I decided to keep this to myself for just a little while. I sat there for a long time, thinking about this incredible creature that was my mom.

Do not leave this world with any regrets. My phone buzzed again, shaking me out of my thoughts, and Steve's number popped up again. I reached down and was about to accept the call, but instead I pressed decline. I scrolled through my contacts and searched for Matthew Carlson's number. Before I could think about it, I tapped on his number and it began ringing. My heart was pounding so loud I was sure the people in the next area could hear it.

"Hello?" I heard Matthew say.

"Matthew? It's Reagan. I've decided to come."

Chapter 6

She's going to come, Matthew thought to himself. He couldn't believe she was going to come. He knew it was a long shot when he had first contacted her, but he had to try for his dad. He sat down in his mom's kitchen and opened up a beer. He had been at the hospital the majority of the day as his dad had test after test trying to figure out what was causing this latest infection.

To see his dad so fragile and so weak was just a shock. His whole life his dad had been so strong and in control of everything. He had seen his dad cry only twice in his life, when he lost his own dad and then years later when he lost his mom. He had lost so much weight since he began chemotherapy a year ago. He looked like the shell of a man that he once was. Matthew could remember the night his father had called him in Colorado to tell him the news. He had been sick for some time, almost like a flu he couldn't shake. Matthew worried about him, but he was so far away with his own family and career that he couldn't do much for him. He would never forget the words coming through on the other end of the phone, "Matthew, I have some bad news. I had some tests done, and the results came back. I have cancer."

Cancer, cancer, cancer: the words seemed to echo through the phone. His dad handed the phone to his mom, and she went on to describe the type of cancer, treatment options, and prognosis. But Matthew did not hear one single word after the word "cancer." He sighed and took another long drink of his beer.

He thought he'd better call home to check on his wife and kids. He'd been gone about three weeks already. He had an older son who was eight and twin girls who were five. They had a little trouble getting pregnant the second time, and his wife Sarah had been put on a small dose of fertility drugs. Within three months, they were pregnant. When they went for the first ultrasound, the technician called in the doctor. He was very worried that maybe they had lost the baby. But after a few moments, he pointed at the screen and said, "Here is baby one." Baby one?? He and Sarah looked at each other. "As opposed to baby zero?" he had jokingly asked, not quite getting it yet. "As opposed to baby two," the doctor smiled.

Six months later, healthy twin baby girls were born. They named one of them Madison after the university where they'd met. The other was Margaret after his wife's grandma; they called her Maggie. Sarah was a saint to let him go while she stayed home to take care of the three kids by herself. Well, she had a lot of help as her family lived nearby. That was the main reason they had moved to Colorado. They were married shortly after college and bought a starter home. After a few years, they sold it for a pretty nice profit and purchased the home they lived in now, relatively close to Sarah's parents. He was originally from Wisconsin but really didn't mind the move, and he loved living in Colorado. He also knew that his mom and dad would eventually retire to Florida, so he didn't need to stay for them.

Sarah was extremely close to her mom, and he wouldn't be surprised if her mom was living with them for a while. When he told her he thought he would have to take a leave from his job as a financial representative, she didn't hesitate to tell him to go and take care of his dad. She was a reading specialist at one of the local elementary schools, and he knew it was a lot for her to juggle her job, the kids, and the house. Thank God school would be done soon and she would have the summer off to be at home.

He did not tell her about the conversation he had with his dad about Reagan. Jonathan had asked him not to tell anyone, including Sarah. Matthew grabbed another beer from the fridge and called her cell phone.

"Hi," she answered.

"Hi, honey. How are you?"

"I'm fine. Everything's fine," was her typical answer. He knew she didn't want him to worry about home during this time and that she would tell him only if anything fairly serious came up.

"How are Brendan and the girls?" he asked.

"No problems," she responded, "How is your dad?"

"He's holding his own right now. He is having a lot of tests done to see what is causing him to have all these fevers. He's fighting some kind of infection, but they can't figure out what," he responded.

"You sound tired," she replied.

"Well, it's a lot of long days at the hospital and also helping my mom through all of this."

"I know, honey. You are a wonderful son. I'm sorry you have to go through this alone," she said tenderly. "Maybe we should come out there?"

"No. The school year is almost over, and I know you have a lot to do. Plus the kids have a lot of end-of-the-year activities that I don't want them to miss. You'll be flying out here soon enough," he said. Then there was a long, silent pause. They both knew what he meant by that.

"Well," she said breaking the silence. "We really miss you, and the kids are drawing you pictures all the time."

"I miss them a lot. Are they home right now?"

"They're at the neighbors playing right now," she responded.

"Okay. Well tell them I miss them and I'll talk to them soon. Maybe we can FaceTime before they go to bed," he offered.

"Sure, we'll talk to you later. Love you," she said.

"Love you too," he said and hung up the phone.

He sat there thinking about Sarah and their marriage. He had never cheated on her and had never even thought about it. He loved her and their life together and really wouldn't change a thing. The kids and her were his whole world, and he couldn't imagine leaving her for someone else. Granted, his dad hadn't left his mom, but obviously something very powerful had happened between him and Reagan. Matthew would have been in high school when the affair happened.

He tried to think back at that time in his life, but he really couldn't remember his dad acting differently or his mom and dad fighting or anything. He was very involved in sports and other clubs and just being a high school kid. If his dad was gone a lot, seeing Reagan, Matthew never noticed since he was probably gone a lot too. Did his mom know something was going on? The only question he asked his dad after he told him about Reagan was, "Did Mom know?" Dad had responded very strongly with a "No, she never knew, and she never will."

He heard the door open, and his mom walked in and set her things on the counter. She usually stayed to eat dinner at the hospital with his dad. Not that he was eating very much these days, but they had eaten dinner together every night of their whole married lives, usually while watching *Jeopardy!* and *Wheel of Fortune*. So to them, this was their way of keeping some normalcy in their new routine, which was anything but normal. She saw Matthew sitting at the table with two empty beer cans and said, "Did you eat anything, Matthew?"

"I was just going to heat up some of that chicken casserole from yesterday," he said, getting up from the table.

"Oh, Matthew, sit down, honey. I will get it for you," she said heading toward the fridge. His mom still treated him like a little boy at times, but he had to admit it was still nice to be taken care of. She set down a steaming hot plate of food in front of him, and they began to talk about the day's events at the hospital.

"Any word on the test result since I left?" he asked while beginning to eat.

"No one came back to the room after you left. I'm sure everyone's gone home for the day," she said with a sigh.

"They'll figure it out, Mom. We have to stay positive," he said.

"I'm trying, but as he's getting weaker, it is getting harder," his mom said with tears in her eyes. He continued to eat quietly, not knowing what to say. In his heart, he knew what these test results would say . . . that the cancer had spread. He just couldn't bring himself to say those words out loud. He knew the family had to remain hopeful, but at the same time they needed to be realistic. That was a difficult combination to maintain. He knew his father's death was inevitable, but there was still that small part of him that thought maybe he would pull through this, or at the very least, they would have a few more years together.

Matthew cleaned up the dishes, and his mom sat down to watch some evening programs. There was such sadness in her movements, and nothing he could do or say would take that away. Matthew stepped outside and sat down in one of the comfortable patio chairs. His mom and dad had purchased a really nice home for their retirement years, and now his dad wouldn't even get to enjoy them. They hadn't even lived in Florida two years when the cancer diagnosis came. Fucking sucked.

Well, at least he was going to fulfill one of his dad's last requests . . . at least he hoped so. Now he had to pray that all went well and Reagan really would come like she said she would. He had told his dad he was still working on his last request but didn't give him any details. He didn't think it would be wise to tell him that she said she would come in case it didn't work out. He didn't want his dad worrying or thinking about it. He wondered what had happened between them twenty years earlier. This obviously wasn't just a one-night stand or some little fling he'd had.

Matthew looked into the Florida night sky thinking about a woman he never even knew existed but who his dad felt so strongly about that he made it one of his last wishes to see her.

Chapter 7

I had never lied to Steve. Oh, sure, the occasional little white lie when I pretended to like a gift he bought, like the time he bought me this hideous dress that I would never wear in a million years. The kind of gift that makes you think to yourself, *Do you really know me at all?* I had to pretend I liked it and then "discover" a small flaw in it so I could return it. I had never cheated on him. I'd never even come close. I didn't think fantasizing about the Croatian doctor from *ER* really counted.

But now I was going to be telling one whopper of a lie. The kind of lie that probably ends marriages, but I was going to do it. So over the course of the next few days, I began figuring out how I was going to get to Florida for a few days. I had to come up with a reason to go that would not involve many people and that Steve wouldn't become suspicious about. Sure, no problem. It had to be believable, and I knew I didn't have much time.

After letting Matthew know that I was going to come, I asked him how much time he thought his father had left. He obviously didn't know for sure, but I asked him to describe his father's overall condition so I could compare it to my mother's and try to gauge a timeline. But, of course, a lot of good that had done me and my family. I was eating a fish fry dinner with her in her kitchen on a Friday night, and the following Friday she died in my arms. However, after talking to Matthew for a while, it didn't sound like the end was all that near. I figured he maybe had a few months left before things got really bad. I told Matthew I would figure out the details and get in touch with him. He simply responded, "Thank you, Reagan."

I taught first grade at an elementary school near my house since I finished my teaching degree over twenty years ago. I was lucky enough to be partnered with an amazing colleague, Kristen, and we have worked together all this time. Over the course of twenty years, we had become very close personal friends. We had seen each other through everything, from the births of our children to the deaths of our parents. She had lost her father several years before I lost my mother.

One morning shortly after talking to Matthew, I was going through my mail at work. I sifted through the many catalogs and advertisements I received for different teaching supplies when I came upon a brochure for a conference on positive discipline. *This could work*, I thought. *I could tell Steve I was going to a conference for school and instead fly to Florida. And while I'm at it, I could buy a piece of swampland,* I chuckled to myself. I couldn't believe I was even contemplating this. The bell rang, indicating the students were ready to be let in, and I headed to the door where my class lines up. I walked out and said good morning to the children, and we started entering the building. My colleague's class followed behind mine, and soon the children were hanging up their backpacks and getting out their daily folders.

"Guess what, Mrs. Bailey?" said one of my first graders.

"What, Bella?" I asked.

"I lost my tooth last night," she said pointing to the new hole in the top row of her teeth.

"Wow! Did the tooth fairy come?" I asked excitedly, using my teacher acting voice. I had many, many roles as a teacher: actor, coach, nurse, referee, psychologist, and occasionally I got some teaching in.

"Yes," said Bella.

"Are you rich as a troll?" I asked her with a grin on my face. Bella giggled and ran to add her name to the lost tooth chart. We began our morning routine of attendance, lunch count, announcements, and the Pledge of Allegiance. Then Kristen and I split our classes into various reading groups and began our morning work. Even though it was May, there were still many skills we wanted to cover before the end of the year. I tried to stay focused on my reading groups, but I kept thinking about this conference. I would probably have to enlist Kristen's help. I knew she would do anything for me, but this was going above and beyond the duty of friendship. I really didn't know what her reaction would be.

We worked through the rest of the morning and then took the kids to recess. I sat on the bench, staring at the swings and biting my fingernails.

"You okay, Reagan? Reagan? Reagan?!" Kristen was waving her hand in front of my face.

"What? Oh, sorry! I didn't hear you," I said.

"Well, that is an understatement. What's going on?" she asked.

"Nothing," I said, but I'm sure my face showed differently.

"Oh, come on, Reagan. I've known you far too long to know that something is up. You've kind of been acting strange for a few days," Kristen said with concern in her voice.

I paused and looked down at the ground for a few moments. "Can you meet for a quick drink after work?" I asked her.

"Woah. Must be pretty serious if we have to go somewhere else. Sure. Let's meet at Marty's. We should be able to sit outside as nice as it is today."

"Okay. Please come with an open mind," I said looking into her eyes.

"Always," she said and looked back at me curiously.

Don't even try, I thought, *You'll never be able to guess what is going on.*

Somehow I got through the rest of the day, but my mind was anywhere but on author studies and fractions. The dismissal bell could not ring soon enough. Finally it was 3:30, and we walked the kids out the front door. Kristen gathered up the kids who go to the after school program and said, "I'll meet you there." I nodded at her and headed back to my classroom.

Normally I stayed to clean up the room and get things ready for the next day. When I first began teaching, there was an older teacher who stayed every night to prepare a complete set of lesson plans for the next day just in case something would happen and she couldn't come in. I was never quite that organized, and thank God Kristen and I had each other to lean on in case of unexpected emergencies.

When my mom passed, I took three weeks off of work and Kristen was a lifesaver. I was off a week before she died while she was in hospice, a week for her funeral, and a week after to get my dad settled. We technically only get three days funeral leave, but I applied for a family leave. You know, three whole days to get over the death of your mom. Three weeks wasn't much better. But it was somewhat comforting to get back to the routine of work and my students. I felt guilty about not being able to be there for my dad as much, but I still had to work.

Today, I did nothing in my classroom. I grabbed the brochure for the conference and stuffed it in my teacher bag embroidered with my name, Mrs. Bailey, a gift from one of my students. I locked my classroom door, headed to the parking lot, got in my car, and drove over to Marty's.

I arrived first, and it was definitely nice enough to sit outside. The hostess led me to a table on their patio, and I ordered two glasses of Moscato. I looked down at my phone and saw a text from Steve.

When will you be home? it said. *Staying after for a bit to work on some projects coming up. Be home in an hour or so,* I texted back. *Wow,* I thought, *the lies are already starting.*

Okay. What about dinner? he texted.

Let's just do pizza and salad, I replied, and then I got the thumbs-up emoji. I saw Kristen pull into the parking lot and get out of her car. I waved to her from the patio, and she made her way over to the table.

"I'm not keeping you from anything, am I?" I asked as she sat down across from me.

"Nah. The kids don't have anything tonight, and they can stay home for an hour or so. Joe will be home soon," she said, referring to her husband. Kristen had two kids also, a boy and a girl who were slightly older than mine. The waitress appeared and set down the two glasses of Moscato.

"Did you want to order any appetizers?" the waitress asked. She had long, blonde hair pulled into a high ponytail and was petite and pretty.

"No," I answered, and we watched the waitress walk away.

"We used to look like that," Kristen said with a smirk.

"Yeah, time flies," I said. We took some long sips of our wine and sat in silence for a few moments. "Speaking of time flying," I said slowly, "can you believe we've been teaching together for twenty years?"

"It's crazy. It seems like yesterday we were meeting in the school library for the very first time," she responded.

"We've been through a lot together. I don't think there is much you don't know about me." I paused and took a long drink. Kristen stared at me. "Until now," I said slowly.

"Reagan, what is going on? Are you pregnant or something?" she asked laughing.

"No," I said rolling my eyes at her. I took a deep breath. "I need a favor. A pretty big one," I said.

"Well, I hope it's not money. I make the same as you, and it isn't much!" she said with another laugh.

"No, it's not money. I need to go somewhere for a few days. I can't tell Steve, so I have to figure out a way to get away without telling him what I'm doing." I pulled out the brochure and slid it across the table.

Kristen looked at it, confused. "Yeah. The behavior conference in Illinois. I got one too . . . tossed it right into the recycle bin. Our district would never pay for something like that. Plus it's over Memorial Weekend. So we are supposed to go to a professional development conference over the holiday," she said rolling her eyes. It's a familiar conversation between us about the injustice of the teaching profession.

"I'm going to tell Steve that you and I are going to this conference, but I'm really going to Florida to see someone," I blurted out and looked at her, not knowing quite how to read her face.

"Okaaay," she said slowly, "Who are you going to see?"

"An old friend," I said quietly.

"Tell me," Kristen said with curiosity all over her face.

"His name is Jonathan," and I began to tell her my story.

Chapter 8

Of course, after that first encounter at the bar, I didn't have to think very long or hard about what to do about Jonathan. My mind told me one thing and my heart and body told me another. I ended up going with my heart and body. The very next time I saw him at work, our eyes locked and I felt electricity run through me. I wanted nothing more than to kiss him again. We began meeting after work at various bars and restaurants and parks where we knew no one would see us. We even went to the movies once. That always stood out in my mind because it was something that a "normal" couple would do.

Sometimes he came to see me on my college campus after I was done with class for the day. I really wasn't even sure how he was pulling this off. I wondered if his wife suspected anything, but he didn't bring it up, so I didn't ask. Instead, we talked about everything, from our childhoods to our future hopes and dreams. He talked about his son Matthew and a son who had died after birth, and, of course, we talked about his wife Karen. They were high school sweethearts who had married fairly young. They had Matthew and then lost a child. They couldn't have any more children after that. They were busy with their separate jobs and interests. They had simply grown apart but never talked about it.

He told me he loved her, but he didn't know if he was in love with her anymore. Their relationship lacked passion and had turned into friendship. He asked me about my family and my plans for after school. I was studying elementary education, so I knew I would be going into the teaching profession. Prior to the bar night, I was casually dating a few guys, but I let all that go when we began seeing each other. I hid this relationship from everyone but my two closest friends. They supported me but did not necessarily approve of it. They didn't want me to get hurt. I didn't want to get hurt either, but I felt powerless to stop it.

We had a strong physical attraction to each other, but I did not let it get very far. We kissed, held each other, and flirted nonstop, but that's where it ended. He wanted more and so did I, but the thought of us beginning a sexual relationship frightened me. Where did we go from there? He began to talk about separating from his wife, and that both scared and excited me. I was falling in love with him, and I wanted to be with him. However, he was quite a bit older, so I wasn't sure how my friends and family would react. I wanted things like a wedding, house, kids of my own. Would I be able to have that with him? I wasn't so naïve that I didn't know that lots of married men get bored . . . the seven-year itch they call it. But I really felt I was more than that to him. We just had this connection that I couldn't explain.

And then one night, things changed. We had been meeting pretty regularly for a few months, and then he asked to meet me at a hotel bar that was far out of town. I drove there with the usual excitement in my stomach and walked into the bar. He was already there and had ordered us some drinks. We ordered dinner and ate and talked.

After we were finished, he looked at me and said, "Reagan, I rented a room here for the night." I stared at him, not knowing quite what to say. "Karen is out of town with Matthew at a baseball tournament, and she won't be home until tomorrow."

"Oh," was all I responded, staring down into my empty glass.

"I just want to be with you, Reagan. Even if it's just to hold you all night." He grabbed my hand and looked at me. "I would never want to do anything you are uncomfortable with. So if you don't want to, just tell me, and I will cancel the room."

I sat in silence, not knowing what to do. I knew I was in love with him, but I also knew this was very, very wrong. The words were echoing in my head to get up and get out of there. But I looked across the table at Jonathan, and my heart pushed those words into a little box and locked it with a key. "Well, we can check out the room, but I'm not promising anything," I said coyly.

He ordered two more drinks, and we stepped into the elevator that stopped at the third floor where the room was. He put the key in, and we walked in and set our drinks down on the small table by the couch. There was a balcony; Jonathan opened the sliding door, and we stepped out into the night air. I turned to him, and he grabbed me and pulled me close. We began to kiss, slowly at first and then more passionately. He grabbed my hand and led me back into the room and pulled me down on the bed. He pushed the hair away from my face and said, "You're so beautiful, Reagan." I smiled, embarrassed, not knowing how to take compliments.

"I'm afraid, Jonathan," I said shyly.

"Afraid of what, honey?" he said looking into my eyes.

"I'm afraid that I will not be able to get over you," I responded.

"And why would you need to get over me?" he asked.

"Well, what are we doing, Jonathan? Are we going to be together? Are you going to leave your wife?" I asked, holding my breath. Up until now, I had been afraid to ask these questions, afraid of the response I would get. I was still afraid, but things were getting real here, and I didn't know what to think. I was hardly a virgin, but I didn't sleep around either. Jonathan looked down at me but didn't respond. "Jonathan, you have to understand. I think I'm falling in love with you. But what am I falling in love with? We can only see each other certain times, my family doesn't know about you, and we clearly can't have a normal relationship."

"Is that what you want? A relationship?" he asked and then said, "We have a lot of issues here. I'm married, I'm older, and I don't see any more children in my future."

"Well, then what are we doing?" I asked.

"Well, I was hoping we were about to make love," he said with a small smirk on his face. I looked at him and began to laugh.

Jonathan got up, freshened our drinks, handed one to me, and said, "Can we just have tonight? Can we deal with those things later?"

I looked up at him and stared into his eyes. Unable to resist him, "Yes," I said softly, and he took our glasses and set them on the table. We began to kiss, and he untucked my shirt from my jeans and pulled off his own shirt. I ran my hands over his arms and back, feeling his warm, muscular skin under my hands. He pulled my shirt off and then unbuttoned my jeans. He pulled them off and lay me down on the bed.

He did not unhook my bra but rather kissed my breasts over my bra, making me arch my back and wanting to unhook it, but he stopped me. He continued kissing me on top of my bra, running his mouth back and forth across my nipples through the material, and slid his hand down my stomach until he reached the silky material that separated me from him. He slid his hand under the material and started feeling me. He brought his face up to mine again and kissed my mouth while making a circular motion with his fingers inside me.

He felt how ready I was, and I could tell that excited him even more as he began kissing me harder and harder on my mouth. He brought his lips to my ear and whispered, "I want you so much, Reagan."

I wanted him too, and it didn't take long before I finished. He pulled the rest of my clothes off me and then pulled off his own jeans and underwear. He climbed on top of me and entered me slowly, all the while kissing me. He began to move back and forth, and I reached up and cupped his face with one of my hands and looked deep into his eyes. He moved faster, and soon he finished, calling out my name. We lay there after in each other's arms. I didn't say it, but I knew I had fallen in love with him.

I didn't tell Kristen all of that, but I told her about the year-long relationship we maintained the best we could. I told her about the feelings we had for each other and the connection we felt. I told her about some of the places we visited and things we did. I told her that it ended, and she did not press for details. I told her about the phone call from Matthew and Jonathan's cancer diagnosis and prognosis and his last wishes. I did not tell her about the rose petals or the letter in my hope chest. Those things were for me.

Our second glasses of Moscato were long gone by the time I finished. I sat in silence, waiting for her to say something.

After a while, she put her hand over mine and said, "I will cover for you."

"Thank you," I said in a grateful voice, and I began to tear up. She called the waitress over and ordered a third glass of Moscato for each of us. Then, we put our heads together and formulated a plan.

Chapter 9

Memorial Weekend was only three weeks away, so I was going to have to act quickly. I would need to tell Steve soon for this to work. Kristen and I had looked into flights for that weekend, and I found one that left the Friday night of Memorial Weekend at 7:00. I would get to Florida in a few hours, and with the time difference should be there by 11:00. I also found a returning flight around 10:00 on that Monday, and I should be home by that afternoon. I was lucky enough on such short notice to find direct flights there and back. We had everything put into place using Kristen's phone. All I had to do was give her the word, and she would book it for me using her credit card.

She, like me, handled all the finances in her marriage. Her husband would never look at the credit card statement. I wrote her a check for the amount of the flight and hotel. Steve barely knew how to write out a check, much less know what went in or out of our account. If something would happen to me, I don't know what he would do as far as our finances.

I had also looked into a hotel and found one near the airport. I had quickly texted Matthew using Kristen's phone to see if that was an okay distance from the hospital where Jonathan was. I wasn't sure what his situation would be like by then, so I wanted to double check if this hotel would work. Matthew said the hospital and Jonathan's home were all relatively close to the airport, so any hotel near there would do. He offered again to pay for the flight and hotel, but it just didn't feel right, so I declined. I didn't want to feel like I was being paid to come there. Kristen and I had already booked the hotel for three nights because they only required a 48-hour cancellation fee, so the hotel was actually all set.

So now I had to talk to Steve. I had to look into the eyes of the man I loved and married and tell him a gigantic lie. A few days later we were cleaning up the dinner dishes and the boys were outside playing basketball. *It's now or never*, I thought to myself and took a deep breath. I started stacking the dishes in the dishwasher, and as casually as I could, I said, "The principal called me and Kristen into her office today."

"Oh, great. What did you two do now?" he said teasingly.

"Nothing bad this time," I said, and with my heart pounding, I continued, "Actually, it's something good. She wants to send me and Kristen to a conference in Illinois."

"Really? What kind of conference?" he asked.

"It's behavior-based," I responded.

"Kid or teacher behaviors?" he said with a chuckle.

"Ha, ha. It's a new positive behavior system for kids," I said.

"So, is she going to get you a substitute for the day?" he asked. He innocently assumed, of course, this was just a one-day thing.

Here we go, I thought and said, "No, it's actually over Memorial Weekend."

"What? What do you mean?" he asked.

"Well, it's a two-day conference, and I would have to leave Friday night and come back on Monday." Did I sound believable? Well, if he looked anywhere at my shaking body, it wouldn't be. I had to remind myself that I was not sneaking off to have an affair.

"You're going to go for the whole holiday weekend?" he asked incredulously.

"Yes. It's a great opportunity, and I could put it on my end-of-the-year evaluation. I really would like to go," I said. We both knew the more I could put on my evaluation, the more bonus pay I was likely to get. We counted on that bonus money to make up for the pathetic salary I received. So I knew if I brought that up, he would be more likely to understand.

"Well, what about up north and stuff?" he asked. Steve's family owned a cabin a few hours away, and we always spent the whole Memorial Weekend there.

"Well, you can still go with the boys. You guys fish and swim the whole time anyway. I don't think I'll be that missed," I said.

"Of course you'll be missed," he stated.

"Oh, sure, you'll miss me there to cook and clean up after you guys," I said in a teasing voice.

"Ha, we can just catch our dinner and cook it over an open fire," he retorted.

"Oh, sure. I'm sure you'll catch the biggest Big Mac in town!" I said and flicked my towel at him. I was glad the conversation had taken on a more playful tone.

He grabbed my arms and pulled me to his chest. "No, seriously, Reagan, you know we would miss you. I think the boys will be disappointed, but if you really need to go to this, then it's okay. I'm just surprised that the district would pay for something like this. You're always saying how cheap they are with things like this," he said.

"Well, actually, Julie said she would pay for it out of our school budget because she had some extra money." Wow! *How was I even making this up?* Now I had to worry that Steve might see my principal some time and bring this up, so I quickly said, "She's not really advertising this to the staff because she doesn't want to cause problems with people getting mad that we're going to this. Lots of teachers want to go to things like this, but no one wants to pay for them." Steve didn't really interact with my principal or staff all that much, but I needed to cover all the bases. I just had to hope it wouldn't come up with anyone other than Kristen. He gave me a quick kiss and then let my arms go.

We finished cleaning up, and the boys came inside, all hot and sweaty.

"Mom, we're dying of thirst," Greyson said dramatically.

"Well how about some root beer floats?" I asked.

"Yes! Yes! Yes!" my youngest shouted excitedly.

Josh said, "Sure, I'll have one." I got out the tall glasses and spoons, the vanilla ice cream, and, of course, the root beer.

I began to scoop the ice cream into the glasses and then said to the boys, "So you know how we always go up north for Memorial Weekend?"

"Yeah," they said simultaneously, not really paying attention to me. They were more interested in how much ice cream I was scooping into the glasses.

"Well, this year I have to go to a conference for school, so I won't be coming with you guys," I said as I poured the root beer over the cold ice cream and we all watched the froth rise to the top. Then I added my special finishing touches of whipped cream and crushed root beer barrels on the top.

"You're not coming with us?" Greyson asked as he spooned whip cream into his mouth.

"Not this year, honey, but you are going to have a guys weekend with Dad and Josh. You guys can fish and swim and eat all the junk food you want. I won't be there to tell you to put more sunscreen on or to get to bed early. Won't that be fun?" I asked, feeling a level of mom guilt that I had never felt before. Must come with lying to your children.

"Yeah," said Greyson, who was really more interested in the float than this conversation. Three weeks away was still a long time in my seven-year-old's eyes.

"Cool," said Josh. He got it, but he's at the age where he's seeking more independence, so this probably did sound pretty "cool" to him. The boys took their floats down to the basement, and I finished cleaning up the kitchen. *So that's that,* I thought to myself. Steve joined the boys, and I moved into our living room and flipped on the TV. *I'm so glad we finished the basement and made a rec room for the boys,* I thought to myself for the millionth time. It gave me a little time at night by myself in the living room to work, read, or watch one of my shows.

Trixie and I curled up with a blanket, and I hit the List button to see the shows I had recorded on DVR. Ironically there was a show I watched called *The Affair,* and I even have the same last name as one of the main characters. I picked up my phone and texted Kristen a thumbs-up sign, which was our code for go ahead and book the flights. She texted back an okay. I would call Matthew tomorrow from school and let him know the details of the flight and hotel. I was really going to do this.

I looked into Trixie's brown eyes and said, "Can you believe this, Trixie Girl? Can you believe what your crazy mom is doing?" She stared back at me and nudged my hand so I would pet her. "Well, since you're the only other girl in the house," I said to her, "you understand, right?" I hoped to God I was making the right decision. I pressed play on the remote and began to watch the show that a little bit resembled my life right now.

When I got to school the next morning, Kristen was already in her classroom getting things ready for the day. She usually arrived before me since I had to drop my oldest off at middle school before heading to my school. Our classrooms had adjoining doors, so I walked through the doorway as I had done every school morning for the last twenty years.

"Mornin'," I said to her.

"Good morning," she said and walked over to her desk. She handed me an envelope and said, "It's all booked. Here is the flight information for you."

"Thanks," I said, looking down at the plain, discreet envelope. It's becoming real now.

"Did you talk to Steve?" she asked.

"Yes."

"Did he buy it?" she asked. A wave of guilt washed over me with those four simple words. I knew she didn't mean to, but it sounded so sinister the way she asked it. She must have been able to tell from the look on my face that I didn't like that question. "I didn't mean it that way, Reagan. You're not going off to have an affair. I know this isn't the most honest thing you have ever done, but I do understand why you are doing it."

"Good, then maybe you can explain it to me," I said with a small smile.

"Are you having doubts about doing this?" she asked.

"Ummm . . . only every second of every day since I decided to go," I responded with my signature notes of sarcasm.

"All I can say is I think if you don't go, you will regret it for the rest of your life," she said, looking at me seriously. I looked back at her, thinking of my mom's last wishes note. I never told Kristen about it, but she used the same words my mom did. Was that a sign? The morning bell rang just then, jolting me out of this conversation.

"Saved by the bell," I said. "Time to get the kids."

"Mrs. Bailey!" shouted Alex excitedly as we walked inside. "I got a new kitten last night. Can I bring it in for show and tell?" And with that statement, I got whirled into my day of teaching.

Usually Kristen and I ate lunch together, but today I went out to my car to make a phone call to Matthew. I found his number in my contacts and called him. He answered right away. "Hi, Reagan."

"Hi, Matthew," I replied back.

"How are you?" he asked.

"I'm okay. How is your dad?" I asked.

"He's still at the hospital. They are continuing to run tests to figure out what is causing this latest infection. He's going to have a procedure done today or tomorrow to see if they can figure out what is going on," he said.

"How are his spirits?" I asked, remembering how my mom was in the last few months of her life. She was hospitalized as well for almost a month trying to figure out what was causing her high fevers all the time. Right before that, I had gone over to her house to visit with her, and when I walked into the house and saw her sitting at the kitchen table, I almost freaked out. She looked so strange, almost yellowish, and she was not making any sense when she talked. It was very frightening. We got her admitted to the hospital that night, and it turned out that she had an extremely high fever caused by the cancer tumors.

"He's okay, but I know he wants to get out of the hospital and come home."

"I know how rough that is, but the hospital is the best place for him. You don't want him home like this. It's very hard to take care of a person this sick by yourself. I was taking care of my mom at home a few weeks before she went into hospice, and trying to figure out pills and oxygen tubes and everything is a nightmare. All I kept thinking was, *I don't know what I'm doing. I'm not a damn nurse,*" I said, hoping I was giving him a sense of comfort. "As much as I didn't want her to enter hospice, I was relieved that someone else would be in charge of all that."

"Yeah, as much as I hate seeing him in the hospital day after day, I know he's in good hands," Matthew said, and I could feel his emotion through the phone. A sense of familiarity came over me.

I'd been down this road before, and as much as every person's cancer journey was different, they were also the same.

I continued the conversation by saying, "I'm calling to let you know that I booked the flight and hotel, so I'm all set to come. I'll be flying in the Friday night of Memorial Weekend late, and I will need to catch a 10:00 flight on Monday."

"That's great, Reagan," he responded.

"Have you told your dad that I'm coming?" I asked.

"Not yet. I wanted to make sure things were set before I tell him. I didn't want to get his hopes up," he responded. I knew I needed to have this conversation with him next.

"Matthew," I said kind of hesitantly.

"Yeah?"

"Well, the flight and hotel are booked, but there is always a possibility this might not happen. I have two children . . . things come up. I can't guarantee that I will be able to do this. I mean, I'm planning on it, but you just never know. As much as I want to see Jonathan, my family will take precedence over this trip. I just want to make that clear." All of a sudden, for the first time since I heard from Matthew, I felt some anger building up. Jonathan had twenty years to make this call, and now when he was on his deathbed, I was the one under pressure to go see him. This felt unfair on many levels.

"I understand, Reagan. I have three children of my own," Matthew said.

"Are you going to tell him now?" I asked.

"Well, we're still a few weeks out from Memorial Weekend, so I think I might wait just a little bit yet. See if we can get him through this latest infection," he said.

And see if I really get on this plane. "Well, Matthew, I better go. I have to get back to work," I said.

"Okay. Keep in touch, Reagan," he said.

We ended the conversation with details about the flight and hotel and plans to speak in a week or so. I rested my head on the steering wheel for a few minutes and thought about all that had happened since the phone rang that Saturday night. Just as I looked up, a red cardinal flew down and perched on the gate directly in front of my car and stared at me almost knowingly.

"Don't judge me, Mom," I said to the bird. "I'm doing the best I can without you here." I got out of the car and walked back into the school to get ready for the afternoon.

Chapter 10

Jonathan blinked his eyes open, and for a few blissful seconds forgot where he was. He then saw the stark white hospital walls and the IV machine dripping fluids into his arm. *Still here but still alive,* he thought to himself. He had been here almost two weeks already trying to figure out what was causing an infection in his body.

He closed his eyes and began to think about what this last year had entailed. He and Karen had moved to Florida almost two years ago to enjoy their retirement years. He liked Wisconsin but preferred sunny, warm days and nights to the bitter cold that comes with living in the Midwest. After they both officially retired from their jobs, they sold their three-bedroom ranch and bought a lovely home in Winter Park. They had several friends who had retired here, and it was something they had always planned on. They had settled in nicely and were surrounded by wonderful neighbors and plenty to do, including a terrific golf country club where he was a very active member. They were able to visit Matthew and Sarah and the kids in Colorado a few times a year, and each winter they came out here for about two weeks.

It was all going well until about a year ago. He had begun to feel very tired all the time and started losing weight unexplainably. He also had a cough he couldn't shake. He thought it was the flu that was going around. Lots of people had come down with it. Karen insisted he go to the doctor, and after some tests, his doctor sat him down and told him he had cancer. It was non-Hodgkin's lymphoma and already fairly advanced.

He stared at the doctor, not quite believing him. Karen began asking a bunch of questions, but he could not hear anything the doctor was saying. The conversation kept going around and around him until finally he got up, walked out of the doctor's office, and went to the parking lot and sat in the car.

He spent a few weeks in a state of denial and disbelief. He refused to talk about it and acted like the visit to the doctor never happened. Karen was the one who took the reins and began calling doctors and treatment centers. She researched everything possible on the internet, and the room in the house they used as a study became a "cancer office." The desk was piled with books and pamphlets. There were notes and phone numbers everywhere. She was facing this head on and forcing him to do the same.

"We're going to fight this," she simply said.

And so the treatments began. She took him to every doctor's appointment and stayed with him through every chemo treatment. She looked up ways to lessen nausea and created solutions for him to rinse his mouth out when they became infected with chemo sores. His fatigue was nothing like he had ever experienced in his life. He did not know it was possible to be this tired. He knew the prognosis was not good, the cancer was too advanced already. They were simply buying him some time. The oncologist never gave him a definite timeline. He kept telling him there were things they could try.

He had been dealing with all of this for almost a year now, and for a while was keeping the cancer at bay. But then he could feel something in his body change, and his doctor, while remaining optimistic, had started to use a different tone when he spoke. Jonathan could tell that he was not responding to the treatments anymore, and he was feeling weaker.

He thanked God he had such a wonderful wife who stood by his side through all of this. He certainly didn't deserve her, but nearing the end of one's life causes you to reflect on things of your past. And he certainly had one big thing to reflect on. Reagan. He'd had a relationship with her a very long time ago. He hadn't seen or talked to her in over twenty years. God, she would be into her forties by now. About a month ago, he decided he had to see her one last time, and he enlisted his son to help him. He knew it wasn't necessarily a fair request, but he had no choice but to ask Matthew to do this. He certainly couldn't do it on his own. He thought back to their conversation.

"Matthew?" he had asked him.

"Yes?" Matthew had answered.

"I need to ask you a favor," he'd said.

"Anything, Dad," was Matthew's response.

"Well, what I'm about to ask you is going to seem very strange, and you will undoubtedly have many questions, but I'm not going to provide you with a lot of answers," he had said.

"Okay. What is it, Dad?" Matthew asked.

"I need you to find someone for me," Jonathan said.

"Who?"

"Her name is Reagan Stills. I'm sure it's not Stills anymore, but I don't know what it is now. She lived in Wisconsin, so she may still be there," Jonathan said.

"Who is she? How do you know her?" Matthew asked with a quizzical expression on his face. Jonathan paused and then looked into Matthew's eyes, not saying a word. All of a sudden, Matthew's questioning look changed to a flash of understanding. Obviously this woman had impacted his father's past in some way. The question was . . . how?

They sat in silence for a few minutes until Jonathan finally said, "I need to see her one more time. It's very important to me, son."

"When was this?" Matthew asked.

"About twenty years ago," Jonathan answered, and he could see Matthew doing the math in his head.

"So this is when you were married to Mom?" Matthew asked, raising his eyebrows. Jonathan didn't respond. "Did Mom know?" Matthew asked.

"No, and she never will," Jonathan said vehemently.

"So you want me to find her?" Matthew asked.

"Yes. I really want to see her. It's really important. It's one of the last things I need to do. Please, Matthew," Jonathan asked, looking into his son's eyes. Jonathan then provided Matthew with a small detail that might help in convincing Reagan to come.

His son looked at him and simply said, "Okay."

Jonathan knew his son would help him and would not ask too many questions. He had asked Matthew whether he found Reagan, and Matthew told him that yes, he had. When he asked how the conversation had gone, Matthew didn't provide many details. He just said he found her and that she was still living in Wisconsin. She was married with two children and was a teacher at a local school. Matthew said he told her about the cancer and his request to see her one last time. He said they were just talking over things right now but hadn't worked out anything definite.

Jonathan knew his son, and he knew he was trying to protect him by not saying too much. He knew Matthew didn't want to get his hopes up that she would come to only be let down in case she couldn't or wouldn't fly out here. He decided not to press for details and simply trust that things would work out.

Reagan had been an employee at the grocery store he managed. He couldn't remember exactly how their relationship began, but they just began talking more and more at work. Every time he saw her at work, he felt this electricity run through him. There was just something about her. She was in college and quite a bit younger. He felt such a strong connection to her that over the course of time he fell in love with her. He loved his wife and his son, but there was something so strong with Reagan that he could not control it. He was very physically attracted to her, but that was not the only thing that drew him to her. He couldn't explain it, but it almost felt as if they were soul mates. He began seeing her whenever he could, but their physical relationship did not start until months after that. Their relationship lasted about a year, and then something happened and Jonathan needed to end it. He knew it would break her heart, but he also knew it was the right thing to do for her. He never saw or talked to her again, but she remained in his thoughts over the years.

After it was over, he was lucky enough to reestablish a connection with his wife. He never told her about the affair, and as far as he knew, she didn't suspect anything. He clearly knew it was an unforgivable, shitty thing to do as a husband, but he wanted to put it in the past and move forward with Karen. He never cheated on her again or ever thought about it.

He often wondered if Karen ever knew, and there were times throughout the affair with Reagan he thought she must have known what was going on. But she never questioned him. She was very busy with her career as a human resources director and kept lots of crazy hours. She also had many hobbies and friends that kept her busy and, of course, Matthew.

They had gone through a very rough patch after their second son Andrew had died shortly after birth. He was born with a heart defect and did not survive long enough for treatment. Karen had had a lot of complications with this pregnancy and birth, and they were advised not to get pregnant again. So he had a vasectomy, they focused on Matthew, and their life went on as normal. They had built a happy life together, and he certainly hadn't gone looking for this. He had never contemplated having an affair . . . until Reagan came along.

Just then a nurse came in, interrupting his thoughts. She checked the fluids in his IV and asked if he needed anything. He asked if any of the test results were back, and she said the doctor was in and making his rounds and would be in to see him shortly. He knew Karen would be there soon, as she spent most of her days in his room with him. He turned the TV on and began watching a morning news program. Not that he really cared what was going on around him. Right now he only had room to process his life. He had envisioned living out his years in Florida with Karen and watching his grandchildren grow up. But now he had to accept the fact that he was going to die . . . and probably sooner than later.

A few minutes later, his doctor appeared in the doorway. "Good morning, Jonathan. How are you feeling today?" Dr. Thompson asked.

"I'm feeling okay . . . a little tired," he answered.

"Is Karen here yet?" he asked.

"Not yet. She is coming a little later this morning," he said. Dr. Thompson sat on the side of the bed next to Jonathan.

"Jonathan, I have the results of the procedure we did the other day. I am afraid the lymphoma has spread to your bone marrow," he said quietly. Jonathan had pretty much expected something like this. The doctor began talking about various treatment options and some things they could try. He explained that first Jonathan would have to get stronger and clear up any infections before they would begin any new type of treatment. He finished going over everything and then asked if he had any questions.

"Am I going to be able to go home?" he asked. Dr. Thompson said he hoped they would be able to send him home in a few days and then plan to begin some course of treatment soon after that.

After the doctor left the room, Jonathan stared at the wall in front of him. He would have to tell Karen and Matthew what was going on. He closed his eyes, and an image of Reagan appeared in his mind. He hoped she would come to see him, but more importantly, he hoped that he would live long enough to see her.

Chapter 11

I am so glad it's Friday, I thought to myself. The week had been crazy, with Kristen and me trying to fit in all the end-of-the-year assessments. There was a lot of pressure to produce good results from these first graders. After Memorial Weekend, which was now a week away, it was all downhill until the last day of school. I had always looked forward to the three-day weekend because it meant that tests were done, scores were recorded, and report cards were completed, and I could just enjoy the rest of the year with my students. But this year's Memorial Weekend was going to be very, very different. In one week, I would be getting on a plane and heading to Florida to see Jonathan. At least that was the plan.

The noon bell rang, and we sent the kids to lunch and recess. I heard much excitement among the boys about playing zombie robots. Greyson was only a year older than these boys, and I could always relate to the things they talked about. I loved the excitement of this age and the fact that they love learning new things. My favorite part of teaching was reading to the whole class and watching their expressions as the story unfolded. As my boys get older and things like Santa and the Tooth Fairy fade—well, they had already for Josh—I was lucky I would always have my students to do those things with.

Kristen brought her lunch over to my room and sat at one of my classroom tables. I grabbed my sandwich from the fridge and sat next to her, and we began to eat as we had done for the past twenty years. "I am beyond sick of turkey sandwiches," I said, biting into my hundredth sandwich of the year. I just didn't have time in the morning to make a more complicated lunch. Sandwiches were just the easiest to prepare, but I knew the boys were sick of PB&J. I always tried to make more interesting lunches in the summer and rarely prepared sandwiches. "Probably just as much as I am sick of these salads," she said back. Our lunch "hour" was about thirty minutes after we got the kids settled, which didn't leave much time for going out to eat.

"So," she said, looking at me cautiously.

"So," I replied, gearing up for this conversation.

"You leave next Friday?" she asked more in a question tone than statement one.

"That's the plan," I said.

"Have you talked to Matthew lately?" she asked.

"Yes, I actually just spoke to him last night. He said his dad was released from the hospital and is back home and actually doing somewhat okay right now," I responded.

"So what's the plan when you get there?" she asked.

"Well, I won't get in Friday night until about 11:00, so I plan to just take a taxi to the hotel. I told Matthew I'd text him when I got settled. He offered to pick me up from the airport, but I told him I'd rather get to the hotel myself," I said.

"And when do you think you'll see Jonathan?" she asked.

"Matthew said he'd work out something for Saturday and Sunday for me to spend some time with him. I'm not exactly sure what he's telling his mom, but he said he would figure it out," I said.

"So, you haven't talked to Jonathan at all then, right?" Kristen asked curiously.

"No. Matthew asked if I wanted to speak to him before I come, but I decided not to. I'd rather just see him in person," I replied. I didn't just want to have some superficial conversation on the phone with him when this reunion was so much more than "catching up with an old friend." We finished up our lunches, and then it was time to go get the kids.

Our afternoon went fairly easily. We always planned fun Friday activities for the afternoon to reward the kids for their hard work all week. This week we planned popcorn and a movie for them. We settled all the kids down with their snack and started the movie. I sat at my desk and began completing some end-of-the-year paperwork.

My phone dinged, and I looked down and saw a text from Steve. *Do you mind if I go out with Kyle and Dan tonight?* Kyle and Dan were his two closest friends from his high school days. They were pretty decent guys, but the three of them sometimes acted like children when they were together. However, I knew Steve would be taking the boys up north by himself the following weekend, so I figured he deserved a night out. *And* also probably the truth about what was going on, but a night out would have to do for now. I texted back a thumbs-up sign. It would be nice to have some time by myself with the boys.

After school, I packed up for the weekend and went to pick Greyson up from his friend's mom who watched him after school for an hour or so. We usually got home about the same time Josh's bus pulled up. As we drove, I told Greyson all about our plans for the evening.

"Cool!" he said excitedly.

We got home, and, as expected, Josh was already there and in the basement playing his video game. "Hi, Josh," I yelled down the steps.

"Hi, Mom," he said back.

"Dad's going out, so it'll be just us for dinner," I let him know.

"Okay," he said.

He probably hadn't even heard a word I said. I let Trixie out and stood outside, sorting the mail I had retrieved. I saw Steve's car heading down the street, and he pulled into the driveway.

"Hi. How was your day?" I asked as he got out of the car.

"Fine. I was ready for the weekend to start. Are you sure it's okay if I go out with the guys tonight?" he asked.

"Yeah, it's fine. I'll do something special with the boys since I won't see them next weekend." I had tried to avoid the topic of Memorial Weekend as much as possible, but now that it was so close, I felt I had to start injecting that topic into our conversations.

"Sounds good," Steve said distractedly, probably thinking about what bars they would hit up tonight. Steve headed into the house to take a shower, and I called Trixie back inside. I started going through backpacks and lunch boxes, clearing them out for the weekend. I always made sure I put permission slips or anything else important in one spot. It would be embarrassing to have a teacher's kid not return something.

After Steve left with a kiss good-bye and a promise not to be out too late, I packed up the boys and we drove over to Dave and Busters. It was hard to get them to eat first, since they were only interested in getting to the video games. They finally settled down enough to eat most of their food, and then they excitedly ran over to the games. I had bought them each a wristband so they had unlimited access for an hour. I walked around and watched them play different games for a while and then parked myself with a soda in a central location called The Parent Zone. I made sure they both knew where to find me, although it would be hard to miss with the bright neon lights that surrounded this area.

The upcoming weekend immediately crept into my mind. I couldn't believe I was really going to see Jonathan after all this time.

I was not sure why I was doing this . . . I certainly didn't owe this to him, and I was lying to my husband and my children.

It was hard to forget how our relationship ended, how much hurt it caused me. About a year after our first encounter at that random bar, I graduated from college. To celebrate, I took a week vacation to Mexico with my two best friends, the ones who knew about my relationship with Jonathan, and boy, did we celebrate! We still talked about all the crazy things that happened that week. Whenever we got together for dinner or drinks, someone almost always referenced our hot tour guide Rosalio who Jenny hooked up with or the skinny dipping we did at the hotel pool.

I didn't have any contact with Jonathan during that week, nor did I talk about him. I think I wanted a break from worrying about where this was going. After the trip, I planned to return to work at the store for the summer until my new teaching position began that fall. I went to the store the day after I got back, excited to see him, only to find out from another cashier that Jonathan had transferred to a new store and would not be returning. She said no one knew the reason why.

We had kept our relationship hidden at work, so I knew no one would suspect I was the reason. She told me that the assistant manager had moved up to manager. I was in shock and did not know what to think. I walked downstairs to his office, not quite believing this had happened. I expected to see him sitting in his office chair working on the weekly budget. The door to his office was closed and locked. Darkness peered through the windows on his door. I went to where my work locker was located, and from across the room I could see a white envelope sitting on top of it. I walked slowly toward it, almost in a dream-like state. I grabbed the envelope and saw his writing on the top. There was one word written on the envelope: _Reagan_. I sank to the floor along with my heart, holding that envelope and staring at it for a very long time. *It's over*, I thought, *it's over*. Greyson ran up to me just then and pulled me back into the present time.

"Mom!" he shouted and then said with worry in his voice, "Mom, are you crying?"

I hadn't realized that my eyes were full of tears. "No, honey. My eyes are just watery. What's up?" I quickly tried to recover.

"Mom, you have to come see this game!" he shouted.

"Okay, buddy. Let's go," I said and got up and followed him to what was a very cool Star Wars game.

That night, after I got the boys settled in bed, I walked into my bedroom and sat down in front of my cedar hope chest. I had bought it shortly after my mom died so I would have a place to fill with her special things. I ran my hand over the dark, smooth wood and traced the outline of the rose that was engraved on the top. I grabbed the small, gold key and unlocked the chest. Lifting up the heavy lid, I breathed in the smell of cedar and what I could only believe was my mom's scent.

I grabbed the white shirt that sat on top and pulled it to me. I breathed deeply and smelled the familiar scent that was my mom. "I miss you so very much, Mom," I said out loud. I started pulling out other things that this box held: photographs, recipes, a Currier & Ives guide to her blue china, and a folder containing articles from the newspaper. She always clipped things out like new recipes, articles about teaching she thought I might be interested in, and gardening tips. I looked over those quickly. Hmm. Not one about pruning roses.

Next I pulled out her prayer card and funeral information. I started to read the beginning of her obituary. I was the one who wrote it. I remember working on it before she even died. How do you capture the life of your mom in one blurb that would be embedded in all the other obituaries that day? I did put a special quote at the end that said, "Mom, you spent your life taking care of our family. You will spend eternity being taken care of by God."

I read that quote over and over again. That was probably the thing I missed most, her taking care of me. Even as an adult, if I got sick or something would go wrong, I would call her. Just the sound of her voice on the other end of the line would make me feel better. I knew she would solve any problem I had, and it would fill me with a sense of relief. How do you describe the feeling of never having that again? It's a problem that never gets solved, a sense of relief that never comes. There is no one on Earth who takes care of you like your mom. I wondered if my children would feel that way about me someday. I hoped so.

I kept pulling things out and setting them on the floor until I got to the bottom of the chest. I saw the letter from Jonathan and picked it up. It was the only thing I had of him . . . I didn't even have a picture. I slowly pulled the letter out of the envelope and began to read it. I was instantly transported back to the locker room where I had sat on the floor twenty years ago and read it for the first time.

Dear Reagan,

This is the hardest letter I will ever have to write. First of all, I want you to know two things. 1. I love you. 2. I am doing this for you. By the time you get back from your trip, I will have transferred to a new store. I do not think it is a good idea for us to contact each other.

Reagan, this has been the most amazing year. I have fallen completely in love with you. You are the most wonderful, beautiful woman I have ever known. I can't describe the connection we have . . . it's something that only comes along once in a lifetime. I will be grateful every day for the rest of my life that I knew you and that we had this time together.

You have a whole life ahead of you. You are beginning your career, and you have so much to experience yet. You are going to find a wonderful man, get married, and have children of your own someday. I cannot give those things to you, and you deserve them.

For the past few weeks, I have been seriously thinking of all of this. It is all I think about. I can't keep going like this. As much as I love you, Karen and Matthew do not deserve this. It would break Matthew's heart if I were to leave, and I cannot do that to him. You will understand when you have children of your own.

I promise that you will get over this and you will be okay. I know you are going to be an amazing teacher. You have worked so hard, and I am so proud of all that you accomplished.

I will never, ever forget our time together. For the rest of my life, whenever I see rose petals in any shape or form, I will think of you. My heart is breaking.

I am loving you enough to let you go.

Jonathan

And that was it. I never spoke to him or saw him again. I quit the store a few weeks later and nannied that summer until the end of August, when I began my teaching position.

I sat there for a while surrounded by my mom's things and then carefully put everything back into the box, but this time I did not bury the letter at the bottom. I placed it near the top underneath my mom's white shirt. I locked the box and put the key away.

I headed into our master bathroom, one of the great things about my house—my own private bathroom—and took a long, hot bubble bath. I lay there under the bubbles and closed my eyes. I wondered what Jonathan looked like now. He had been a very handsome guy when I knew him. Of course, I knew the chemotherapy would have taken a toll on him, and I wouldn't get a true version of what he really looked like. I wondered what he would think about me. I guess I was an attractive woman back in the day. I was tall, thin, tan, and had long, brown, curly hair. In your twenties, everything looks good on you. Well, two nine-pound baby boys are not very forgiving on the body. I was far from overweight, but I certainly could use some toning up. It's funny when you think the "before" women in the Hydroxycut commercials look pretty good.

I got out of the bath and stood in front of my full-length mirror, staring at my body. I had a little more weight around my stomach and hips than I would have liked. I had wrinkles around my eyes and skin that was not all tan and smooth. What would he think when he saw me now? If he was picturing twenty-something Reagan in his mind, he was sure to be disappointed.

I put on shorts and a T-shirt and climbed into bed. I looked at my clock on the nightstand, figuring Steve would be home soon and would probably want some husband-wife time, as he liked to call it. I loved Steve with all my heart, so why was I doing this?

I glanced at the cedar chest and thought about the letter that was now nestled near the top of the box. A fucking "Dear John" letter. That was all I got after all we had meant to each other. Maybe I didn't mean as much to him as he meant to me. Twenty-year-old-doubt was resurrected and dusted itself off inside my soul. Maybe our whole relationship meant nothing to him. Maybe it was just a sexual attraction for him.

But then why would he contact me after all this time? I now knew why I was taking this trip to Florida. I needed to get answers to my questions. I needed to know what I meant to him. In short, I needed to get the closure I had not gotten twenty years ago.

Chapter 12

Jonathan was sitting outside with Matthew on the patio having coffee. Karen had run to the grocery store to pick up a few things. He actually seemed to be functioning okay these days, and he and Matthew were talking small talk when Matthew decided it was time to tell him about Reagan's visit.

"So, Dad, I told you that I found Reagan and had some conversations with her. Well, what I haven't told you is that she has agreed to come out here to see you, and she'll be arriving on Friday night," Matthew said.

He set down his cup and stared at Matthew. "She's coming?" he asked.

"Yes."

"This Friday?" he asked.

"Yes."

"Oh my God," Jonathan said and sat back in his chair with a mixed bag of emotions on his face: shock, relief, excitement. "I can't believe I'm going to see her," he said.

"Well, she's flying in Friday night late, so I'm planning on arranging for you to see her Saturday," Matthew said.

"How are we going to do that?" Jonathan asked.

"I'm thinking of telling Mom that I'm taking you to the baseball game on Saturday. Tampa Bay is playing against the Orioles, and I'll tell Mom I bought tickets. I had actually thought about doing this with you anyway. If you add up the hours for the drive there and back and the game itself, that should buy you plenty of time with Reagan on Saturday," Matthew said, carefully laying out his plan.

"I don't know what to say, Matthew. I can't believe you were able to arrange all of this. I know this isn't easy, but I really need to see her. I appreciate all you're doing for me. Thank you," Jonathan said in a very grateful voice.

"You're welcome, Dad," Matthew said back. He filled him in on the flight and hotel information but made sure to tell him that it could all still fall through. "She did make sure to tell me that if anything came up with her family, the trip would be cancelled."

"I realize that, Matthew," Jonathan said in a thoughtful voice, "Things could come up with me too." Memorial Weekend was now less than a week away, but he knew at any moment he could end up back at the hospital, or worse. They could hear Karen pull in the driveway.

"I'm going to help Mom with the groceries," said Matthew and he stood up, ready to lend a hand.

Jonathan grabbed his arm and looked up at him, "Matthew, you don't know how much this means to me."

"I do know you wouldn't ask me to do this unless it mattered so much, but I can tell you I really hate lying to Mom," Matthew said, looking down at his dad.

"I know. I don't want to hurt her, but I don't want to die never seeing Reagan again," Jonathan said with a determined look in his eyes.

After Matthew went into the house to help Karen, Jonathan sat there thinking about Reagan and their time together. He thought about one of their most memorable times when they drove down to the lakefront and spent hours walking along the water and talking. He felt like he could tell her anything. He loved looking into her beautiful hazel eyes and brushing her long brown hair away from her face. All of a sudden, the sky turned gray and big drops began to appear on the sand and were bouncing off the lake water. Then the sky opened up and it began pouring down on them.

He grabbed her hand, and they ran laughing through the rain all the way back to his car. They jumped into the car and looked down at their soaking wet clothes. There was a moment of silence, and then they began kissing more passionately than they had ever before. They climbed into the backseat and began pulling their clothes off each other in desperation. The rain was pounding down all around them, and the windows were completely steamed up.

She climbed on top of him and held his face in her hands and looked at him, her eyes filled with such love and passion. He knew he would remember that look for the rest of his life. They made love, and he told her for the first time that he loved her. She smiled, leaned over, and whispered in his ear, "I love you too, Jonathan."

After, when she was lying in his arms with her eyes closed, he ran his fingers through her long brown hair and said, "I mean it, Reagan. I love you and not just when we're like this. Our love is so unique it's like . . . like . . ." He stopped, not knowing how to finish that sentence. She didn't respond for a few minutes, and he thought maybe she was even asleep. Then she opened her eyes, looked up at him, and said, ". . . like finding rose petals in the snow." He stared into her eyes and then grabbed her and kissed her like a man who had just found the greatest treasure in the world. He held onto her, not wanting to ever let her go.

They had spent about a year together, seeing each other wherever and whenever they could. The rose petal reference became a part of their relationship. He would leave them for her in unexpected places, never roses but piles of petals. He knew he loved her, and he knew that he wanted to spend the rest of his life with her. But he also knew he had a family that did not deserve what he was doing.

He was torn between the life he had created and a life with this wonderful woman. He could not have both, and he knew he had to make a decision. He just didn't know which one to make.

Until one warm spring evening, when the decision seemed to be made for him. He and Karen were sitting at one of Matthew's baseball games, and Matthew got very hurt. He took a ball to the head and fell over on the ground. Jonathan flew off the stand, ran out on the field, and kneeled beside his son. He was knocked out for a few moments and bleeding from his head, and they rushed him to the hospital. Matthew was in a lot of pain and crying. He ended up having a concussion and needing several stitches. While they waited to be released, Jonathan sat on the side of Matthew's bed in the hospital comforting him about the rest of baseball season.

Matthew was so upset and just said, "Thanks for being there for me, Dad."

"I will always be here for you, son." And looking down at him, he did not see the teenager lying there. He saw his little boy, and knew that he could never leave him. He knew he needed to end it with Reagan. But he also knew he would not be able to end it with her in person. He would take one look in her gorgeous eyes, and he wouldn't be able to do it.

Jonathan knew that Reagan was going to be off of work the following week while she took a graduation trip with her friends. So he contacted his boss and asked for a transfer to a different store that was closer to his home. The boss didn't really ask for further explanation, and he was able to make the switch the week Reagan was gone. He was doing this for both of them, although he knew she might not see it right now.

On his last day at the store, he wrote her a letter and left it on top of her work locker. He packed up the things in his office, walked out of the store, and never looked back. He knew it would break her heart when she found the letter, but he knew a clean break would be best. He never talked to her or saw her again.

Now, twenty years later, he was going to see her. He wondered what she looked like, what her family was like, and how her teaching career went. But most of all, he wondered if she ever thought about him over the years. Well, he was about to find out soon enough. He had to remember to pick up a gift for her, something that would take her back twenty years to a time when they were very much in love. He knew just what to get.

Chapter 13

I stopped by my dad's house on Sunday as I usually did. I knew the week ahead would be busy and then I would be gone the following weekend.

"All set for up north next weekend?" he asked, knowing our typical plans for the holiday. I hadn't yet told him of my plans not to go.

"Well actually, I'm not going up north . . . just Steve and the boys are," I said.

"Why aren't you going?" he asked with a surprised look on his face.

Well, Dad, because I'm flying off to Florida to see a dying man that I had an affair with twenty years ago. That's perfectly normal, right? I thought to myself but of course did not say. My parents did not know about my relationship with Jonathan. I hadn't lived at home during my college years, so they never found out about him. "I'm going to a conference with Kristen in Illinois," I lied.

"For school?" he asked.

"Yes, my principal is sending us there to learn about a new behavior system."

"Over the holiday weekend?" he asked, not quite understanding.

"Yes, it just happens to fall over that weekend. It will be fine. Steve is going to have a guys weekend with Josh and Greyson. They are all excited about it," I said, knowing my dad really wouldn't have a reason to question it.

"Is Rob coming on Saturday?" I asked, trying to change the subject. My brother and his family were coming to spend the weekend with him. I was glad he would not be alone over the holiday. My brothers and I were fairly close, but parents are really the connection that holds siblings together. Now that my mom was gone, we had my dad and his grief to keep that connection going. But after my dad died, then what? How would our relationships change?

"Yes, he's coming about noon on Saturday and staying through Monday."

"What are you guys going to do?" I asked.

"Oh, Rob made all sorts of plans for us. There are a bunch of festivals and parades that he wants us all to go to."

"That will be nice . . . I bet you're excited to see the kids." My brother Rob had two boys and a girl, and my other brother Ryan had a boy and a girl. It did make the holidays interesting when we got together with all the kids. My boys loved seeing their cousins, and we always had a lot of fun gathering at my mom and dad's house.

My mother especially loved Christmas, and each of the kids would have a huge pile of wrapped presents from floor to ceiling to open. It took us hours to get through everything. We always referred to it as the "marathon." I truly think they had more fun seeing their pile and opening everything than actually playing with the toys. My brothers and I had the same experience when we were kids, and she kept it going for her grandkids. They all couldn't wait for "Santa's" visit at my mom and dad's house.

My memories of Christmas would forever include ripping open the wrapping on a new Strawberry Shortcake doll and running down to the basement with my brothers to sneak her homemade chocolate-covered candy out of metal coffee cans she thought she had hidden so well.

Things were painfully different now, although my brothers and I tried to keep up with her traditions. It was a lot of pressure, and not something I was confident I could continue for the rest of my life.

That last Christmas she was alive, I stood in front of their tree by myself for a few moments. Boxes and wrapping paper were strewn all over the floor. I could hear all the grownups in the kitchen drinking coffee and talking. The kids were in the back room playing with some of their new toys. I stared at the tree, my face reflecting back at me on one of her large glass ornaments.

And I knew.

I knew this would be her last Christmas. Holidays would be forever changed after this one. That was a hard pill to swallow. I walked into the kitchen and caught her eye as she sat in her usual seat, coffee mug in her hand. I looked directly into her eyes and offered a small smile. Her expression changed as she stared back at me, and I knew she knew what I was thinking. But there were no words said about it.

"Anything you need done, Dad?" I asked, clearing my head of past holidays. I ended up taking him to the grocery store to get some things for the upcoming week. After my mom died, he began driving less and less. He would still drive to the store and my house, but that was about it. He would not drive at night at all anymore. I parked the car, and we headed inside the store. His movements were slower than a few years ago. It was amazing the physical toll that grief takes on your body.

We began going up and down the aisles. It was so painful to watch him try to pick out food that could make a dinner for one. My mom had done all the grocery shopping and cooking, so he was pretty lost the first few months. He had gotten a little better and would make the occasional pot of spaghetti or chili. We went to the frozen food aisle, and he picked out some single-serve frozen dinners. I stared at them in the cart, feeling like the world's worst daughter, vowing again to make sure I spent as much time as I could with him this summer and making sure he had home-cooked dinners.

Several weeks before my mom died, we were having a conversation, and she started to cry. I asked her why she was crying, and she said, "I'm leaving you with Dad. I was going to take care of him." I told her he would be okay, and she said, "You're going to have your hands full." She knew how hard this was going to be, and I knew sometimes I would be angry with her, not for dying but for doing everything for my dad her whole married life. This was all he knew, life with my mom. I don't think he even remembered life before her.

We finished shopping and drove back to his house. I carried all the bags in and began helping him put everything away. I opened up one of her cabinets, and on the inside of the door, there was still a yellow post-it with a phone number to one of my mom's doctors written in her cursive. I stared at it, thinking of her standing in her kitchen, jotting this number down and sticking it there, close to the phone, so she could call to make her appointments.

"What's wrong, Reagan?" my dad asked, breaking me out of my trance.

"Nothing, Dad," I said. *Everything's just fine except my mom is dead*, I shouted in my head. But I couldn't say that. I couldn't let him see my grief. I don't think I had ever really even broken down in front of him since she died because I had to hold him together. Didn't he ever think I missed her too? He never really acknowledged that besides losing his wife, I had lost my mom!

I went outside to check out the yard and garden, still not sure what the plan was for all of that. The yard was looking pretty decent, thanks to my dad's constant watering with the sprinkler. He hadn't touched the garden or the rose bush area. Despite the lack of care, the rose bushes seemed to be coming up nicely, and soon we would see a variety of blooms in red, white, pink, and yellow.

I sat down in the grass in front of the roses and touched the stems in front of me. I closed my eyes, and a breeze hit the air just then and surrounded my face. I lifted my face to the sun and breathed in the fresh, spring air and remembered one of my last conversations with my mom. Sometimes I don't want to remember, because the pain can nearly knock me over, but this time I let the memory come.

She had been in hospice a few days but was starting to lose the ability to speak. I knew she could still hear me; the hospice doctor had told us that her hearing would be the last thing to go, so we should be careful what we were saying in front of her. She was pretty much unable to respond at this point. Her eyes were closed most of the time, and I knew she was in and out of consciousness.

I was in the room alone with her and sat down next to her on the bed. My brothers had taken my dad to the cafeteria to make sure he had something to eat. I looked down at her lying in the bed in her yellow cotton nightgown. She had worn a nightgown to bed every single night of her life. Unlike me, who pretty much slept in my clothes every night since I was too lazy to change out of them. I was frightened to be alone in the room with her, and I wasn't sure why.

So I did what I knew how to do best and that was talk in uncomfortable situations. I have had lots of practice at that in my twenty years of being a teacher. I have had to sit across from parents and tell them that their child was showing signs of autism. I have had to sit with inebriated parents at conferences and tell them we would need to reschedule when they were in a better state. I had to listen to one parent bash another parent because they, of course, were not the cause of their child's issues. So I looked at my mom and began a one-sided conversation, a conversation that tied me to my past.

"Mom, I know you can hear me. I have some things I want to say to you. First of all, I'm so sorry, Mom, that this has happened to you. You are too young for this, and you do not deserve this. I don't know why God is calling you Home so soon, but He is, and we have to trust there is a reason. You don't have to hang on here for Dad. I will take care of him. He'll be okay. He's going to miss you like crazy, but we'll get him through. You were the best mom in the world to me. You took care of me for my whole life, and now I will have to do the same for Dad and my family. You were a great example of what a mom should be. I only hope I can be as half as strong as you were in tough situations. I will try to follow your example."

I stared at her peaceful face and continued, "There are so many things I'm going to miss about you, Mom. I will miss shopping with you even though we both actually hate shopping and really looked more forward to going to lunch than trying on clothes. I will miss calling you and chatting about the boys. I know when I'm sick or worried, I will miss having your shoulder to lean on. I will miss knowing you are a phone call away. I will miss planning the holidays with you and creating menus for special celebrations. We are all going to miss your cooking.

"I am sad for not only the things I will miss now, but I am sad for all the future graduations, weddings, and births you will miss. I am sad for Josh and Greyson to lose their most loved grandma when they are still both so young. I know I should be grateful that you got to see all the grandchildren born, but it's just not enough. I will miss you every second of every day for the rest of my life. There will not be a moment that I am not thinking about you," I said, realizing how many levels of grief there are. I was grieving the immediate loss of her being in my life, and I was also grieving the loss of all the future events she would miss.

I stopped and put my hand on top of hers and felt the warmth of her skin against mine. I was born and raised Catholic and had received all the traditional sacraments growing up. I believed in God and Jesus, and until now, I never questioned Heaven and the afterlife. I wanted to believe that she was going to place called Heaven, and I wanted to believe that I would see her again. I hated my doubt, but I couldn't help what I was feeling. Would I ever see her again? And even if I did, what would it be like? My heart began to physically hurt, and I had to control myself so I wouldn't break down sobbing in front of her.

I wanted to know there was something else after her time on Earth, so I said, "Mom, I want you to do something for me. I want you to leave rose petals in unexpected places only for me to find. Maybe you could put some petals in the snow by my house in the middle of winter. Please, Mom, so I know you're okay and so I know I'll see you again."

I sat for a few more minutes. She hadn't stirred at all up to this point. I squeezed her hand and said, "I love you, Mom. Watch over the boys for me." I started to walk away when I saw her move a little bit. She opened her eyes slightly and then raised her arms straight up from the bed to give me a hug. I leaned over, and she wrapped her arms around me. I hugged her and hugged her in that yellow nightgown. That was the last time she moved. She died the following night.

When Matthew called to tell me Jonathan wanted to see me, I couldn't believe he brought up the rose petals. Jonathan had remembered that after all these years. I remembered the first time I had mentioned the rose petals to him. We had just made love, and Jonathan told me for the first time that he loved me. It was a moment filled with tenderness and passion, and I never felt more in love with him. Jonathan and I were trying to describe what our love was like, how special it was. I told him that our love was as unique as finding rose petals in the snow. That was in my more poetic days, but it stuck with us. Jonathan left me rose petals everywhere.

I opened my eyes, and the rose bushes in front of me seemed to stare straight at me. It had been almost a year and a half, and I still had not found any rose petals from her. "Mom, where are you?" I said out loud, "Where are the rose petals?" There was nothing but silence.

I stood up and thought to myself, *I'll just have to keep looking.* I went back inside to hang out with my dad for a little bit before heading home.

"What were you doing, Reagan?" he asked.

"I was just checking out the yard a bit, seeing what needs to be done. You'll have to decide soon if you want to plant a garden."

"I know," he said in a sad voice.

I had never spoken to anyone about the rose petal request I'd made to my mom. There were only two people in the whole world I had ever discussed rose petals with. One person was already gone and had not filled my request yet. The other person was dying, and I hadn't spoken to him in twenty years. These two very important people in my life had never met in this world, but they had one very important thing in common. They had both broken my heart.

Chapter 14

After I left my dad's house, I decided to take a drive by some of the places that Jonathan and I had spent time together. I drove by a park we used to go to and the woods nearby that we took walks in. I drove by the hotel where we spent our first night together. The hotel was still there but was now run under a different name. I sat in the parking lot staring at the building remembering that night, the night we made love for the first time. Then I drove down by the lakefront where we walked along the water that one rainy afternoon.

I parked my car and got out and began taking a walk, retracing the steps I had taken twenty years ago. I sat on some nearby rocks and pulled my knees up to chest, staring out at the waves. For some reason, visiting these places gave me a sense of purpose for this trip. I needed to remember our relationship and what we had meant to each other. Otherwise, what the hell was I going out there for? *It was real,* I thought to myself. It was as real as any love I had ever known. I stared at the waves for a long time when suddenly a sailboat appeared on the horizon. The sail was quite large and had orange-and-blue stripes that formed a bright contrast against the dark water. Lake Michigan wasn't exactly known for its crystal-blue water.

I shielded my eyes against the sun and watched that sailboat travel further and further away. I remembered something I had read at the hospice during my mom's four-day stay there. There was quite a lot of literature on death and dying, but there was one piece of writing that stood out to me that I had thought of from time to time since her death. The author was describing dying, comparing it to a sailboat going out of the sight on the horizon. And just as we can no longer see it, there are people on the other side ready to welcome it, saying, "Here she comes."

On my mom's last day at the hospice, there was a difference about her. She was completely unresponsive to us but breathing very heavily in her sleep. The warmth had already seemed to have gone from her body. It was like her body was still there but her soul no longer was. Her sailboat had left us, and she was on her way to a new horizon. I watched the sailboat until I could no longer see it, and then I walked to my car and drove home.

That night, after I had given Greyson a bath, read him a few chapters in the book we were reading together, and tucked him into bed, I sat at the table making a list of the things Steve would need to take up north. Josh was still up and working on some homework that was, of course, due the next day.

"Josh, do you want me to help you pack for up north?"

"Mom, seriously, I am old enough to pack my own clothes." It was so strange to think that Josh was almost a teenager.

"Well, make sure you pack sweatshirts and sweatpants. You know how cold it can get up there at night," I said.

"Yes, Mom, I know," he said rolling his eyes. I generally did all the packing and planning, and it was a weird feeling knowing I wasn't coming along. I wrote down all the things I thought they would need: pillows, sleeping bags, lanterns, bug spray, swimming and fishing gear, clothes, and food.

"Whatcha doing, Reagan?" Steve said, coming up behind me and peeking over my shoulder.

"Just writing out everything you need to take along," I said and then asked, "What should I buy for food?"

"Oh, just some stuff for burgers and hot dogs . . . keep it simple."

"Okay," I responded and started to make a separate list of everything I needed to get at the grocery store. I needed to make a Florida list but could hardly do that with my family around. What do I even need to put on that list? A huge bottle of wine, I chuckled to myself . . . to get through this.

"I can't believe you're not coming with us," said Steve, "It sure will be different without you there."

"I know, honey, but school will be out soon after that, and we'll have tons of time together as a family," I said, really trying to make myself feel better about this whole situation.

"What time are you guys going to leave?" I asked.

"Oh, I forgot to tell you I was able to take a half day on Friday, so I'll pick up the boys around noon and then head to the cabin," he answered.

"Oh, that's good. You'll avoid rush hour after work then," I said, making a mental note to let the schools know that the boys would be getting picked up early. Steve would not think to do that.

"What time will you be heading out?" he asked.

"I'm going to come home after work and finish packing. Kristen is going to pick me up around 5:00, and then we'll drive to the hotel where the conference is at," I lied. She was picking me up at 5:00 but only to drop me off at the airport for my 7:10 flight. She was also going to pick me up from the airport on Monday and bring me home so it would just look like she was driving me home from the conference. I was glad Steve and the boys would already be gone by the time I got home from school on Friday so I wouldn't have to face them before heading to the airport.

After Josh had gone to bed, Steve and I headed downstairs to relax and watch some TV before getting ready for the work week ahead. I sprawled out on the couch with my legs over his lap in a familiar position. He began running his hands up and down my legs, something I absolutely love. We stayed like that for a while, watching some dumb survival reality show.

"So, are you looking forward to this weekend?" he asked.

"Well, it will be a lot of meetings I'm sure. I'm guessing more work than play," I answered with my eyes on the TV. I hoped he wouldn't start asking a bunch of questions that I would have to fumble answers to.

"Where are you guys staying?" he asked.

Shit. I should have had an answer prepared, but I didn't.

"Umm, you know what? I can't think of it right now . . . one of the major chains though. Kristen has all the information and she's driving, so I didn't really check it out that much," I got the words out, trying to sound believable.

"Well, how would I reach you in case of emergency?" he asked.

"Just what emergencies are you planning on having with my two children?" I said in a horrified voice.

"Nothing, I hope," he said back with a mischievous look on his face.

"Well, you can always call my cell and I'll give you all the flight and hotel information," I said and then realized what I just did. Shit. Stay calm, I told myself.

"The what?" he asked, looking at me.

"What did I say?" I asked, pretending that I was so engrossed in the TV show that I didn't even know what I'd said.

"You said the flight and hotel information? What flight?" he asked.

"Oh, I didn't mean that. I don't know why I said that. I meant the hotel and conference information," I said, hoping he dropped it. Thankfully he did, and we finished watching the show and headed up to bed.

We climbed in on our respective sides and set the phone alarms for the next day. He pulled me close to him and said, "Hello, my love." This was something he usually said when he wanted something from me. "What can I do for you?" I asked, knowing full well what the response would be. He began to kiss me, and I knew where this was leading.

I pushed all thoughts of Jonathan and this trip out of my head and focused on the man I had married. I wasn't going to let this interfere with my relationship with Steve. That would be completely unfair, and I was already doing enough damage. I had to remind myself yet again that I was not going off to have an affair with Jonathan. I was going to say good-bye to a sick, dying man and to get closure on the past.

I wrapped my arms around Steve and looked into his eyes and told him how much I loved him. He held me tight and said, "I love you too, Reagan." I had one final thought before I gave myself over to Steve: *How on earth did Jonathan do this to his wife? Did he really love me that much?*

Chapter 15

I would be getting on a plane in four days to go see Jonathan, and there were only four people in the whole world, including myself, who knew this. Driving to work that Monday morning, new doubts and worries crept in as Friday drew closer. Which was probably a welcome change to my brain, which was tired of mulling over the same worries and doubts. What if one of the kids got seriously hurt at the cabin? What if the plane went down? Steve would have no explanation of what I was doing on a flight to Florida. Of course, Kristen would be there to explain why we were not in Illinois. Yeah, that would make it all better. My children would grow up without a mother, never understanding why I had to take this trip.

"That's it, I can't go," I said out loud. I thought, *When I get to work, I am calling Matthew and telling him the whole thing is off. This was absolutely the worst idea I have ever had in my life. What was I possibly thinking? Heading to Florida because of a phone call?*

Screw this. If he wanted to see me so bad, he could just drag his ass on a plane and fly to Wisconsin. He could just bring his chemo drugs with him. His wife wouldn't question him flying to the Midwest to see the woman he had an affair with on her twenty years ago, right?

I pulled into the school parking lot and pulled my cell phone out of my bag. I scrolled down until I got to Matthew's number. I would just call him and tell him something had come up with my family. He'd understand. And even if he didn't understand, who cares? I didn't owe this to him or Jonathan. I got a Dear John letter twenty years ago, and now I was the one flying across the country to see him, putting my marriage at risk? What the hell kind of deal was this?

I would just cancel the flight and the hotel and tell Steve the conference was cancelled. I would go up north with the boys and relax and put this whole thing behind me. I would never think about it again for the rest of my life. I was about to press Matthew's number to call him, and then I stopped. Only one problem: it would probably be the only thing I think about for the rest of my life. That would not be fair to my family.

I rested my head on the steering wheel and stared down at my phone, the screen lit up with Matthew's number ready to be dialed. Another teacher pulled in next to me and tapped on my window. "You okay, Reagan?" Samantha, the music teacher, asked. I gave her a nod indicating I was okay and pointed to my phone like I was in the middle of an important call.

I stared straight ahead trying to decide what to do. I felt like my heart was literally being pulled in two places. Damn him for putting me in this position. Was I really going to be able to pull this off? And what were the consequences to him? Even if his wife found out, he would be dead soon. I couldn't believe I thought that. Just added another notch next to Reagan's name on the list of Who is Going to Hell.

I started playing with my mom's wedding ring that sat on a chain around my neck. I slid it back and forth and asked, "What should I do, Mom?" There was no answer, of course, and I knew the answer must come from within myself.

I knew she never would have struggled with a decision like this because she never would have put herself in this type of situation to begin with. She had met my dad in high school, they dated a few years, got married, and began having kids. She went from a kid to a wife to a mom and just took care of her family. She felt that was her job, and she never in a million years would have gotten involved in something like this.

My dad's words echoed through me: *You are your mother's daughter.* How so? I needed to figure that out. I needed to go to Florida. I closed my phone and headed inside the building to get ready for the school day.

Chapter 16

Matthew set the coffee and doughnuts on the counter and waited patiently while the young girl rung him up. He had just run a few errands and decided to bring a treat back. Things moved so much slower in the South. It was as if everyone had all the time in the world. Growing up in the Midwest, Matthew knew that was not how things were everywhere. Where he grew up, everyone was always in the world's biggest hurry, and heaven help the driver that was going slow in the fast lane. He paid for his items and headed back to his parents' house.

Reagan would be coming in four short days, and he knew his dad was getting anxious to see her. He already had talked to his mom about taking him to the baseball game on Saturday. He told her he wanted to spend some father-son time with him. She wondered if Jonathan was strong enough to go, and Matthew convinced her that it would be fine. She was a little reluctant but eventually agreed that it would be okay. So things seemed to be all working out. He drove though his parents' quiet neighborhood and turned the corner. His parents lived near the end of the block. That's when Matthew saw them: the flashing lights of the ambulance that was parked in his parents' driveway.

He raced down the street, threw his car in park, and flew into his parents' house. His dad was lying on the couch, and there were two paramedics surrounding him.

"What happened? What's going on?" Matthew shouted in a state of panic. His dad's eyes were closed, and he was wearing an oxygen mask. One guy was taking his blood pressure and another one was talking to his mom.

"He started having some chest pain and trouble breathing, Matthew," his mom said. "I didn't know what to do, so I called 911." He looked at his mom's tear-streaked face and went over to hug her.

"Come on, Mom. Let's head into the kitchen and let these guys do their job." Matthew put his arm around his mom's shoulder and gently led her to a kitchen chair.

"He was fine after you left. We were sitting outside and he started complaining of some chest pain. Then he looked like he couldn't breathe. I got him into the living room, and he lay on the couch. He didn't seem like he was getting any better, so I called for help," his mom said through tears.

"You did the right thing, Mom. I'm sure he's going to be okay," Matthew tried reassuring her.

The paramedics came into the room to talk to them. "He's stable and we've gotten his breathing under control. We are going to transport him to the hospital, though, to get him checked out by his doctor."

"Okay," said his mom, and she went to get some things to take with her. Matthew watched as the paramedics picked up his dad and laid him on the stretcher. The oxygen mask was still on, but his eyes were open now. He looked at Matthew, and Matthew could see the panic in his eyes. He held up four fingers. He knew what his dad was trying to say. Reagan was coming in four days. He leaned over and told his dad not to worry about it.

Matthew and his mom followed the ambulance to the hospital. His mom went to the front desk to take care of the paperwork. After his dad was admitted and settled in his room, Matthew and his mom went in to see him. The oxygen mask was off, and he looked a lot better than he had a half hour ago. The color was back in his face, and he seemed to be breathing normally.

"How are you feeling, Dad?" Matthew asked him.

"I feel okay. I feel like I can breathe now," Jonathan said, looking relieved.

"Are they going to run some tests, or what?" Matthew asked.

"Dr. Thompson is actually here right now, so they said he'd be in to see me in a bit," Jonathan said.

Karen sat in the chair by the bed. "You gave me quite a scare, Jonathan," she told her husband.

"I know, honey, I'm sorry I scared you. I honestly feel okay right now," he answered.

His mom stood up. "I think I'm going to find a cup of coffee. Matthew, do you want anything?"

"No, I'm okay, Mom. Thanks, though," he answered her. She left the room, and Matthew went to sit by the side of his dad's bed. "Are you sure you're okay, Dad?" he asked again.

"Yes, I feel totally fine."

They were silent for a few moments. "I'm going to call Reagan, Dad, and let her know what's going on," he said.

"No, Matthew, please don't. I want her to come. I need to see her . . . I need to tell her some things before it's too late. If you tell her I'm in the hospital, she's going to cancel everything."

"Well, let's wait and see what the doctor says, okay?" Matthew said, trying to keep his dad's hopes up.

His mom came back to the room, followed by his dad's doctor. Dr. Thompson was an excellent oncologist with a wonderful bedside manner. Matthew was glad that his dad had been in such good hands out here in Florida.

"Hello, Jonathan. How are you feeling?" he asked in a kind voice.

"I'm doing a lot better," Jonathan answered truthfully. Dr. Thompson came over and examined him. "Well, I want to take a chest X-ray and run a few tests to see what's exactly going on here," he explained.

"How long do you think I'll be here?" he asked, and Matthew was the only one who heard the real question in his voice.

"Well, let's see what the test results show, and then we'll go from there. I'll be back to check on you later this afternoon," Dr. Thompson said and then stood up and walked out of the room.

Jonathan looked at his family and said, "I'm not staying here again."

Matthew's mom said, "Honey, we'll just have to see what the tests say."

"The tests are going to say that I'm dying. I already know that," Jonathan said. The three of them sat in silence after that comment.

Around noon, his mom decided to go to the cafeteria to get something to eat, and Matthew went with her. His dad had fallen asleep, and they wanted him to get some rest. His mom began chatting with one of the ladies behind the counter. She had gotten to know some of the people here pretty well since she'd been here so much with Jonathan.

They both ordered a soup-and-sandwich combo and sat down at one of the tables to eat. He was glad to see his mom eating; she needed to keep her strength up for what was coming.

They ate for a few minutes, and then his mom said, "Matthew, I'm so glad you're here. It would be so hard to go through all of this alone."

"Of course, Mom. I wouldn't want to be any other place. You and Dad took care of me my whole life, and now it's my turn to repay the favor." Then Matthew decided it was time to bring something up that he hadn't yet, something he and Sarah had talked about. "Mom, I just want you to know that when all of this is over . . . when Dad's . . ." he stopped, not able to finish the sentence.

He took a deep breath and tried again. "When the time is right, I want you to know that you are welcome to come live with us and the kids. Sarah and I already talked about it, and she is fine with it," Matthew said, looking at his mom, not quite knowing what her reaction would be.

His mom looked straight at him, "Matthew, that is a very kind offer, and I appreciate it. Your dad and I have talked about this too. I'm not going to make any definite plans for at least a year. I really like living in Florida, and I have lots of supportive friends around me."

"But Mom, I don't want to leave you out here by yourself," he said and felt himself choking up.

"I'll be okay, Matthew, and you have your own life to live. Your dad and I have had a wonderful marriage, but we always kind of had our own paths in life. There is no doubt I will miss him every single day, but I know I can survive this," she said. They finished their lunches and deposited their trays. "I'm heading back up to the room to see if Dad's awake yet," she said.

"I think I'm going to give Sarah a call," Matthew said, knowing who he was really about to call.

"Okay, honey. I'll see you in a bit," his mom said, and Matthew watched her walk toward the elevators.

Matthew headed outside and found a bench to sit on. He pulled out his cell phone. He knew his dad didn't want him to make this call, but he felt that Reagan deserved to know what was going on. If his dad was going to be stuck in this hospital, he didn't see how he would be able to arrange for her to see him. He knew it was the middle of the day, but he took his chances and hoped that he would be able to reach her at school.

He found her number and hit send. Her cell phone was ringing, but then it went to voicemail. He hesitated, not knowing if he should leave a message or not. After her heard her greeting, he said, "Reagan, it's Matthew. Something's come up I need to talk to you about, so please give me a call when you get this message. Thanks. Bye."

He headed back inside the hospital and took the elevator up to his dad's room. Jonathan was awake and staring at the TV. His mom sat in the corner chair, flipping through a magazine.

"How are you doing, Dad?" he asked.

"Fine. I'm just waiting, as usual," he said.

"They're coming to take him for a chest X-ray soon," his mom offered.

"Oh, good. Hopefully that will give us some answers," Matthew stated, and then his phone buzzed. He looked down and saw Reagan's number appear on the screen. Shit. Of course she would call back right now.

"I need to take this call. I'll be right back," Matthew said, and he felt his dad's eyes on him all the way out the door. Matthew walked down the hallway to one of the visitor rooms and shut the door behind him, praying he would have good reception. He quickly answered his phone and said, "Hello, Reagan."

"Hi, Matthew, I just got your message. I took the kids to art class, so I have a few minutes to talk. What's going on?" she asked.

"I wanted to let you know that my dad's in the hospital," he told her.

"Oh, no. Is he okay?" she asked with genuine concern in her voice.

"Well, he had some trouble breathing, and my mom had to call 911. The paramedics came and transported him to the hospital. We're waiting on some test results." Matthew didn't realize how upset he was about all of this until now. He could hear his voice shaking as he spoke the words out loud and wondered if she could hear it too.

"I'm sorry, Matthew. It is a roller coaster ride, isn't it?" she said in an understanding voice.

"Yep. And I want to get off," he said and felt himself choking up again.

"Hang in there, Matthew. Sometimes things aren't as bad as they seem," she said, trying to offer some comfort.

"Well, I just wanted to let you know in case he has to stay here. I mean I'm not sure about your trip out here now," he said.

"Matthew, don't worry about that. Just take care of your dad. I am very familiar with the ups and downs of this process. Keep me informed, and we'll take it day by day," she said with the voice of someone who clearly had been through this.

She spoke to him about some of the things that had happened with her mom. "It's like I was always waiting for the axe to fall. It's very exhausting sitting vigil day after day after day. I spent hours researching everything that lung cancer entails. I would analyze survival statistics and compare every case to my mom's. I would tell myself she surely had more time and that she could be part of the percentage that survived at least five years after diagnosis. It's a living hell," she said, and Matthew understood completely.

"Thanks, Reagan. I'll be in touch," Matthew said and hung up the phone. He stared at the vending machines in front of him that were supposed to offer some tangible comfort to the families waiting for news. Somehow he didn't think peanut M&Ms were going to make this situation better. One of the hardest things about all of this was that he didn't have anyone he could talk to about this, not even his wife. He was alone on this mission, and it sucked.

Matthew headed back down the hall to his dad's room.

"How's everything at home?" his mom asked.

"Fine," was his short answer as he stared at the floor.

"I bet the kids miss you," she said.

"Yeah, but they're pretty busy with the end-of-the-year activities," he said, not wanting his parents to feel an additional burden of him being out there. His dad stared at him, not saying anything but saying everything at the same time.

When his mom went to the bathroom, Jonathan turned to him and said accusingly, "You called her, didn't you?" Matthew said nothing. "I asked you not to call her," his dad said angrily.

"I know, Dad, but if you're going to be here, she has a right to know. She has a family, and if she has to cancel this, I want her to have time to do that," Matthew explained.

"Is she still coming?" Jonathan questioned him in a worried voice.

"We decided to take it day by day and see what happens," he said.

"We?" his dad asked, raising his eyebrows.

"Well, whatever. She's the only other person in the world that I can talk to about this situation. It's not like this is easy for me, Dad. You're dying. I'm trying to fulfill one of your wishes. I'm having conversations with a woman I've never met who, frankly, you cheated on Mom with. I'm away from my family. What the fuck do you think this is like?" Matthew said, throwing his arms up in the air, giving a visual image of the weight on his shoulders. It was the first time he had gotten truly angry at his dad since his cancer diagnosis. They sat in silence.

Finally his dad asked, "What's it like talking to her?"

"What do you mean?" Matthew asked.

"Well, one of the best parts of our relationship was all the conversations we had. She was a great listener, and we were able to talk about anything," his dad said with a little smile, clearly remembering something.

"Yeah, I can see that," Matthew agreed. "It's pretty comforting talking to her. She went through all of this with her mom, so she understands where I'm coming from," Matthew said.

"Her mom is gone?" he asked.

"Yeah."

"How long?"

"About a year and a half."

"What kind did she die from? Do you know?" his dad asked.

Matthew paused. He looked at his dad and in a quiet voice said, "Lung cancer."

"Hmm. Well I guess you two will have a lot in common. Plenty to talk about if she actually flies out here," Jonathan said and turned to stare out the window.

Matthew had no idea how to respond to that.

"Is her dad still alive?" he asked Matthew.

"Yeah. I get the feeling she spends a lot of time taking care of him," Matthew said.

"That sounds like something she would do," his dad said.

Karen came back to the room, so they dropped the conversation. They spent the afternoon watching the hospital TV and waiting for the doctor to come. Finally, late that afternoon, Dr. Thompson came back.

"How are we doing?" he asked the room.

"Okay," they all mumbled.

"Well, Jonathan, we have the results of your chest X-ray. You have a touch of pneumonia, which is not uncommon in your stage of lymphoma. We're going to start you on some strong antibiotics to try to kick it out of you," the doctor explained.

"Will I have to stay here?" Jonathan asked.

"We're going to keep you here overnight for observation, and we'll see how things go tomorrow. Okay?" he said.

"Okay," Jonathan answered. What choice did he have?

"Well, that's not too bad, Dad. Hopefully we can get you out of here tomorrow," said Matthew.

"I hope so," he answered.

Matthew and his mom stayed through early evening with Jonathan and then decided to head home. Matthew watched from the doorway as his mom hugged and kissed his dad. He knew they loved each other, but there was something that changed in his dad when he spoke of Reagan. His eyes lit up, his expression changed, and he looked twenty years younger. It was as if the cancer didn't exist. If only he could bottle up what his dad was feeling during those moments and use that in his treatments. Unfortunately, there was no way to bottle memories.

Chapter 17

I set the phone down on my desk, and my heart sank in a tangled mixture of disappointment and relief. Jonathan was back in the hospital, and this trip might be cancelled.

Kristen came over to my desk just then and asked, "What's wrong, Reagan? Who was that?"

"That was Matthew calling from Florida. There was a complication with Jonathan, and I may not be going now," I said.

"What kind of complication?" she asked.

"He had some trouble breathing and ended up back at the hospital," I explained.

"Didn't he just get home?" she asked.

"Yep. I remember that with my mom too. The last few months she was in and out of the hospital. I think she spent more time there than at home," I said sadly.

"So now what?" she asked.

"I'll just have to wait and see. If he ends up having to stay there, I'm not going to go. How am I going to see him at the hospital with Karen there all the time? It will never work," I said.

"What are you going to tell Steve?" she asked.

"Well, I'll just have to tell him the conference was cancelled and I'll go up north with them," I said, shrugging my shoulders.

"How are you going to feel about that?"

"Like how I've felt this entire time . . . that I can't believe this is really happening."

After work, I had planned to stop at the nearest department store to do a little clothes shopping. I couldn't remember the last time I went shopping. Oh, yeah. When I had to go pick out funeral clothes. Unlike most women, I really did not like clothes shopping, and neither did my mom. We would go once in a while together, but both of us hated trying stuff on. I still had the receipt in my hope chest from the last time we went shopping. Ironically, it had been over Memorial Weekend a few years back, and I had bought some clothes for a trip to Disney World with my family.

Now here I was, shopping for clothes for yet another trip to Florida, albeit very different circumstances. I knew the trip might get called off, but I still decided to go to the store. *I can always use new clothes for work*, I thought to myself.

After I picked out a few things, I went to the dressing room to try them on. I stepped inside and locked the door behind me. I stared at the empty chair in the corner where my mom always sat. She would come in with me and offer her opinion on things I tried on. I remembered us laughing at certain outfits, and if one looked particularly ridiculous, she would always say, "You look like you just got off the boat." I could literally hear her saying that as I tried on a flowered dress, and I started cracking up. "That's a no, huh, Mom?" I said out loud.

I kept trying on outfits and having conversations with her as if she were really there. The people in the next room probably thought I was nuts. It's strange how I think about my wardrobe now. It's divided into two sections: clothes I had before my mom died and clothes I bought after. I don't know why I started thinking about it like that. For some reason, it made me feel sad when I wore something new, and I'd think about the fact that she'd never see me in it. It's funny the things that bother a person.

I ended up buying a sleeveless black dress that was pretty

slimming and a few other pieces as well. Pretty good for me, as I usually ended up buying nothing. I headed home with my purchases and started thinking about seeing Jonathan for the first time after all these years. I tried to picture what our first encounter might be like. What would we say to each other?

I had to remind myself that this trip might not happen. I also had to remind myself that I was not meeting him for a date or for a romantic encounter. He was a very sick, dying man. He would be changed, not only from the last two decades but from the disease itself. Cancer was not forgiving. It took your hair, the color in your skin, your weight, your energy, your life. Jonathan and I would not be walking along the ocean having a romantic conversation, nor did I want that.

I pulled in my driveway and knew Steve and the boys would not be home yet. I had talked to him the day before and had asked him to pick up Greyson so I could stop at the store. He reminded me that Josh had a track meet. Ugh. I dreaded those. Hours of watching other kids to see him run for two minutes. I decided to be a bad mom and skip the meet.

Trixie greeted me at the door, and I went to my bedroom to set my things in the closet. I texted Steve and asked how much longer they would be at the meet. He texted back *about an hour*. I texted back telling him not to let Greyson eat too much junk food, knowing how much he loved the concession stand. If I had to add up how much money I had spent on popcorn and Sour Patch Kids over the years, I could probably feed my family for a month.

I decided to get dinner going. I looked for something quick and easy since it was after five already. I pulled out the things to make spaghetti and started boiling noodles and browning meat, planning to eat about six. I threw together a quick salad and placed some frozen breadsticks on a cookie sheet. After I stirred in some sauce and everything was simmering, I poured myself a glass of wine and sat at the table. Trixie jumped on my lap, hoping for some delicious handout. "Sorry, Trix. I've got nothing for you right now." I loved to watch her eat spaghetti noodles, though. It was a very *Lady and the Tramp* experience.

I alternated between taking sips of wine and petting her soft, black fur. "Well, Trixie Girl, I'm supposed to be taking this trip in a few days, but now Jonathan is in the hospital," I said to her. She was a great listener. "I don't know whether to feel relieved or disappointed that I might not be going." I stopped petting her, and she looked up at me as if to say, "Probably a little bit of both."

I really didn't know what to think. I wished I had a sign from my mom. I had never even really dreamed about her other than dreams where she played an insignificant role. I read about these things called "visitation dreams," but I had never gotten to experience one. They were supposed to be very different than normal dreams. The deceased person was supposed to appear younger and healthier, and the dream was supposed to feel very vivid and real. Visitation dreams were supposed to give the person dreaming them a sense of comfort. I had asked her several times to appear in one, but it had never happened. So no rose petals and no visits at night. *Where the hell was she?*

Steve and the boys came home just then.

"Hi, Mom," said Greyson, running up to me all excited.

"Hi, buddy. How was the meet?" I asked.

"Great. Dad bought me Sour Patch Kids. I ate the whole bag," he said, grinning.

"Fantastic," I said, giving Steve "The Look."

"Hi, Josh. How did you do?" I asked.

"Pretty good. I came in third in the 200-meter dash and second in shotput."

"Great job," I said, hoping that was the right response.

"Dinner is just about ready. Why don't you guys go wash your hands?" I asked. I started to plate the noodles and pour the steaming sauce on top.

"What are we having? Oh, spaghetti! Yum!" Greyson shouted excitedly. We all sat down to eat, and the conversation turned to the upcoming weekend. "Did you buy us lots of snacks, Mom?" Greyson asked, shoving noodles into his mouth.

"I actually haven't bought all the groceries yet, but I'll get to the store in the next day or two," I told him. We continued talking about all the things they would need to bring along. I made mental notes to myself, knowing I'd be the one doing most of the packing.

It was a nice night, so after dinner, I took Trixie for a walk around the neighborhood. Greyson joined me on his bike, and I kept yelling ahead to stop at each corner. Again, being the worrier that I was, I always had this vision of him falling off the bike or a car coming around the corner unable to see him.

When I was a kid, my mom did not accompany me on each and every bike ride. I didn't even wear a helmet back then. I just got on my bike and went with a "see you later" to her, and that was it. I knew things were a little different back then, but she never seemed to worry that something would happen to me. How did she go through life like that, and why hadn't I inherited that gene?

"Watch me, Mom," Greyson said as he did some little trick with his bike. He sure was growing up and becoming less and less my little boy. He was only five when my mom died. So little. For God's sakes, I think I was about thirty when my grandma died.

Watching Greyson just then, I thought about the last memory I had of my mom with the boys. About two weeks before she died, we went over to my mom's house to make apple pies. We always called her "the best apple pie maker in town." I knew time was running out, and I wanted to make sure the boys had some quality time with her. She showed them how to carefully peel and slice the apples. She taught them how to pinch the crust around the edges. What was that called? Fluting? One of the last pieces of advice she gave my children was "to leave out the nutmeg and double the cinnamon." She could not stand nutmeg. Josh kept a picture of him and my mom slicing apples on his nightstand. Greyson kept a picture of her tending to the flowers in her garden on his dresser. She was such a wonderful grandma to all her grandchildren. She never missed a special occasion, whether it was a birthday or the first day of school. She sent a card and a gift for everything! I once again felt the loss this was bringing to all of our lives.

The morning after my mom died, I had to wake the boys up and tell them that their grandma was gone. Josh didn't say too much, but I could see in his face the sorrow he was feeling. It was my little five-year-old who turned to me and said, "But Mom, you don't have a mom anymore." That one simple sentence brought me to a halt. I'd spent months taking care of her, worrying, praying, and hoping, and now that was all gone. But she was gone too. I didn't have a mom anymore.

We continued our walk/ride around the blocks of our neighborhood, and my thoughts turned to Jonathan. I wondered how he was doing and if he was going to be released from the hospital. It's a tricky road, this cancer business. It's a constant vigil, and the worrying was almost worse than the actual results or news. I remembered waking up every morning with a constant pit in my stomach. I almost couldn't bear it when our house phone rang, knowing it was going to be my dad with an update. I especially enjoyed those phone calls in the middle of the night where I was awakened at, like, three in the morning to hear my dad say an ambulance was en route to his house.

I felt for Matthew, knowing what he was going through and

what was still to come. I wanted to see Jonathan, of course, but part of me wanted to go out to Florida to meet Matthew and tell him, "It's going to be okay." Now I might not get the chance to do either of those things. I needed to channel my "inner mom" and not worry about what would happen. "What will be, will be," I could hear her saying to me. I just needed to believe that.

Tuesday and Wednesday passed, and I did not hear from Matthew. It took everything in me not to call him, but I had no idea what was going on and I didn't want to bother him. I kept myself busy getting the boys ready for their trip up north. Thursday morning, I woke up and my first thought was, *Am I getting on a plane tomorrow or not?* I knew if Matthew didn't call me today that I would have no choice but to call him and see how Jonathan was. Thankfully I didn't have to make that choice. On my way to work that morning, my phone rang and I saw Matthew's number pop up.

"Thank God," I said with relief and picked up the phone. "Matthew?" I said into the phone.

"Hi, Reagan," said Matthew in a voice I really couldn't read.

A terrible thought ran through my mind just then that maybe Matthew was calling to tell me that Jonathan had died. "Hi. How . . . how's your dad doing?" I asked with my heart pounding.

After filling me in on the last two days, he said, "He's doing a lot better now. He was released from the hospital yesterday, and the pneumonia seems to be clearing up."

"That's great news, Matthew," I said, and I couldn't believe the relief that washed over me just then. "So am I still planning the trip out there?" I said and held my breath.

"Yes," he responded.

"You think your dad will be up for this?" I asked.

"Yes, for sure. He was very concerned that you might call it off. He wants me to assure you that he is fine," Matthew said.

I paused and then said, "What about you, Matthew? Do you still think this is a good idea?"

"I know that this is probably my dad's last wish, and I want to make it come true for him. I'm not sure if the whole baseball game idea is going to work out now on Saturday because that might be too long to be away. I don't know if my mom will be on board with that," he said unapologetically.

"Sure. What's the plan then, Matthew?" I asked.

"I'll figure it out," he said.

"It's kind of hard to hear you. Where are you?" I asked.

"I'm actually at my dad's country club hitting a few rounds of golf. I'm here alone so I finally had an opportunity to call you and let you know what's going on," he said.

After we hung up, I went inside and headed to my classroom. Kristen was already there as usual and came over to me right away.

"Did you hear from Matthew?" she asked.

"Yes, I just got off the phone with him," I responded.

"Well? What's up?" she asked, looking at me with raised eyebrows.

"Well, what's up is that Jonathan had pneumonia but he's home now and doing much better," I said back.

"So are you still going down there?" she asked.

"That is still the plan. We're going to talk tomorrow morning, and if all is well, I will be getting on the 7:00 flight," I said to her. She nodded and walked back to her classroom to start preparing for the morning. I went to my desk and began checking my work emails. I stared at a family photo that was framed and perched on the center of my desk. My husband and my two boys stared back at me silently, asking me why I was doing this.

I had the answer to this question. "I have to do this for me, you guys. Please understand," I said to the questioning eyes in the photo.

Tomorrow night I would be getting on a plane and traveling over one thousand miles to face my past. The question I didn't have an answer to was: What would this do to my future?

Chapter 18

Jonathan was so relieved to be home relaxing in his recliner in front of the TV. There was just nothing as comforting as being in your own house. Each time he went to the hospital, he feared he wouldn't make it out of there. He was definitely feeling much better, and the pneumonia was pretty well cleared up. He wasn't set to go back to the hospital for at least a week, so he wanted to enjoy his time at home. He could hear Karen bustling about in the kitchen making them breakfast. The smells of bacon and coffee filled the air . . . the smells of home.

Jonathan's mind turned to the thought that Reagan would be flying in to Florida tomorrow night. He could hardly believe that he was going to see her after all these years. Now he had to figure out a way to spend some time with her. Karen would never let him go on an all-day baseball outing now.

"Jonathan?" she called from the kitchen.

"Yes?" he answered.

"What time do you think Matthew will be back?" she asked.

Matthew had gone to the country club where Jonathan belonged to hit a few golf balls. Matthew deserved some time to himself.

"Oh, probably not for at least an hour or so," Jonathan said. He turned his attention to the morning news program in front of him. He thought of an idea just then, a way to get out of the house. The same guilty feeling he felt twenty years ago now just washed over him. How many times had he lied to Karen about where he was going or where he had been in order to see Reagan? He cleared his head and thought, *I'm not having an affair. Nothing, absolutely nothing is going to happen with Reagan. I just need to see her.*

"Jonathan, it's ready," his wife called. Jonathan turned the TV off and climbed out of the recliner. He felt a little weak when he stood up, so he quickly sat back down and took some deep breaths. The doctor had told him he needed to take it very easy and gain some of his strength back. He got back up and headed into the kitchen, where he was surprised to find an empty kitchen table. He looked through the patio door and saw that Karen had set everything up on the table outside. He stepped through the glass doors into the Florida sunshine and sat down at the table. She had set out ham-and-cheese omelets, bacon, toast, fruit, orange juice, and coffee.

"Wow, Karen. This looks delicious. Thank you," he said to his wife.

"You're welcome. You need to eat . . . doctor's orders," she said in a determined voice. He filled his plate and began to eat.

"Well, this is way better than hospital food," he responded in a teasing voice.

"I certainly hope so!" she responded. They ate in silence for a few minutes.

"How are you feeling this morning?" Karen asked him.

"I'm doing okay. I felt a little weak earlier, but I think that's to be expected," he said.

He took a few more bites and then decided to jump into the conversation that was on his mind. "So, I think I'd like to go to the country club with Matthew and maybe hit a few golf balls," he said, looking at his plate.

"Oh, Jonathan, do you really think that is the best idea right now? You need rest," she said.

"I am resting. Golfing isn't all that strenuous," he said.

"Oh, really. People have had heart attacks and died on the golf course, you know," she said.

"Great! That will save me from dying from this cancer thing I have," he replied with a smirk.

"Really, Jonathan. That isn't funny," Karen said and then swatted him on the arm.

"Seriously, Karen. I want to go and spend the day there just hanging out with Matthew and playing golf. It might be the last time I get there," he said seriously. Karen didn't say anything for a few moments and then relented.

"Well, we'll see how you're feeling the next couple of days and then decide."

Matthew came home just then and joined them on the patio.

"How did it go, Matthew?" he asked.

"Fine. I just played a few rounds and talked with some of the guys there. It's a really nice place," Matthew said.

"Yes, I love it there. I was thinking maybe by Saturday, if I'm feeling better, you and I could go there and spend the day," Jonathan said, looking at Matthew in the eyes, sending him the real message. He could tell Matthew got the message by the look on his face and the understanding in his eyes.

"Sure. I think that's a good idea, Dad. Saturday is supposed to be beautiful," Matthew said, nodding his head.

Karen piped in just then stating, "IF he's feeling okay. We'll have to see."

"Sure, Mom," said Matthew and began piling food on his plate. "This looks great. I'm starving," Matthew said, diving into his breakfast.

After breakfast, Jonathan decided to take a short walk around the neighborhood.

"Just be careful, honey," Karen said with a worried look on her face.

"I'm fine. The doctor said a little walk here and there is fine. I'll take my cell with me, and I'll be back in a little bit," Jonathan said and headed out the door. He liked walking around the neighborhood and wished again he had a dog to take on walks. It wouldn't be fair now, though, leaving a dog to wonder where his owner went. It was just so surreal sometimes knowing that he was going to die soon.

He ended up walking to a nearby park and sat down on a wrought iron bench near the entrance. He sat down and realized that the short walk had zapped the energy out of him. It was like he was an eighty-year-old man instead of sixty-two. His eyes filled with tears as he once again thought of everything he had already lost and was about to lose to this horrid disease. Cancer just didn't give a fuck if you had a wife or children or grandchildren or retirement years to enjoy. Jonathan wiped his eyes and leaned back on the bench and took in his surroundings. How many more times would he get to appreciate nature and all its offerings?

He started thinking about his decision to find Reagan. When he knew he did not have a lot of time left, he started asking himself questions. And one of his questions was if he could see anyone in the world before he died, who would it be? He didn't even take a millisecond to come up with the answer. Reagan's name came into his mind as bright as if it was lit up on a billboard. He didn't know if it would be possible, but now he was on the verge of seeing her again. Once she was here, he would have about forty-eight hours to make things right with her. He probably didn't deserve this bucket list wish, but if she was willing to come, then he was going to take the chance.

Jonathan's phone buzzed, and he didn't have to glance at the screen to know that Karen was calling to check on him.

"Hi, honey," he said into the phone.

"Hi. Just checking on you. Are you okay?" she said.

"Oh, yes. I stopped at the park, and I'm just hanging out in the sunshine," he said.

"Okay. I wanted to make sure," she said.

"I'm heading back now," Jonathan said. He hung up the phone and stood up and stretched. He began the short walk home, thinking of all he wanted to accomplish in the next couple of days. Something in his heart did not feel right, not physically but emotionally. What was it? He turned the corner and saw Karen outside watering the flowers.

He stopped a little ways back and just stared at her. His wife of almost forty years. She would be the one to plan his funeral and bury him. She would be the one to come home to this empty house and have to pick up the pieces alone. He watched her for a while and noticed how lovingly she cared for the flowers. It took him a few minutes, and then he put his hand to his aching heart. He was so busy trying to repair his past that he forgot to take care of his future. He should not only be trying to make things right with Reagan. He should be making things right with Karen. But he knew he would never tell her about his relationship with Reagan. What good would that do now? He did not want to inflict any more pain on her than she was already enduring.

He slowly moved up the walk toward her.

"Hi, honey," she said.

"Hi. How are the flowers coming?" he asked.

"Good. How was your walk?"

"Fine. Why don't we sit in the back for a while?"

She looked at him and then said, "Sure. I'll grab us something to drink."

Jonathan headed to the back and settled into one of the patio chairs; Karen brought out two glasses of iced tea. They sat drinking and talking about the yard. He had imagined years of them doing this, talking, planning, enjoying retirement. Now they only had months . . . if he was lucky. Jonathan fell silent.

"What it is, honey? You feel okay?" she asked him.

"Yeah. I feel fine. I'm just . . ." his voice trailed off.

"Just . . . ?" She looked at him, encouraging him to continue.

"I'm just so sorry for all of this," and with that, he broke down.

"Jonathan, you don't need to be sorry. This isn't your fault. It's life. Life doesn't always go the way we planned," she said, putting her hand over his.

With his hands pressed to his face, he finally said what had been bothering him for so long. "I'm sorry I wasn't a better husband," he whispered.

"What are you talking like that for? You are a wonderful husband. Now stop that," she said.

"Karen, I . . ." and Jonathan looked at her. He had no other images in his mind other than this woman he had been married to for almost forty years. This woman who he had two children with, one they raised together and one they buried. This woman who he had spent his life with and who had stood by him through everything cancer related and not. "I just want you to know how very much I love you and what a wonderful wife and mother you are."

She reached over to hug him, looked into his eyes, and said, "I know how much you love me, Jonathan. I love you too. And with all we have been through, there was never any doubt about whether or not we loved each other. It's all going to be okay."

"It is?" Jonathan asked, wiping his eyes.

"Yes. You just need to clear your heart before you go," and with that, Karen got up and went into the house.

Jonathan sat there wondering the same thought he had twenty years ago: *Does she know?* He knew then there would never be a conversation about Reagan between them. He would never know if

Karen knew then or now what was going on. But maybe he didn't need to know. He just needed to clear his heart.

Chapter 19

I looked out the window of the airplane as it touched down. After we were safely on the ground and the attendants did their thing, the doors opened and people started departing. I grabbed my carry-on from the overhead and headed down the middle aisle of the plane. I walked through the walkway and stepped out into the bustling Orlando airport. I slowly walked away from the people I had shared this flight with and started down the escalator to the exit signs. *I have to get a taxi,* I thought.

As I stepped off the escalator, I saw something in the distance. A sign that said Reagan. It was covered in rose petals. And then I saw who was holding the sign. Jonathan. I dropped my bag and ran toward him shouting his name. Before I could reach him, a security alarm went off, and people were pulled in all directions. Jonathan was out of reach by this point, and I tried to get to him, but he was swept away in a crowd. I screamed his name, and the alarm kept blaring and blaring.

I heard someone shouting my name, "Reagan! Reagan!"

"What?" I shouted and sat up.

"Turn your alarm off!" said Steve. I reached over and hit the stop button on my phone alarm. I fell back onto the bed and shook my head clear of airports and security alarms. "I'm going to hit the shower first, okay?" said Steve.

"Sure," I told him and burrowed under the covers. Holy shit! What a dream! Tonight I would be getting on a plane and heading to Florida. That part was not a dream.

After Steve got out, I jumped in the shower, beginning my morning routine as usual: shampoo, conditioner, shave, body wash. It's amazing how something so out of the ordinary could be taking place in less than twelve hours, but here I was starting out like any other normal day.

I started making a mental list of everything I still needed to pack. I had spent last night packing my clothes, but I still needed many of the toiletries this morning. I got out of the shower and pulled on jeans and a simple T-shirt. I would be going on the airplane in these clothes, so I wanted to be sure I was comfortable enough.

I could hear Steve getting the boys breakfast, so I decided to quickly apply my makeup and dry my hair. After I was done, I threw the rest of my makeup and hair supplies into my travel cosmetic bag and placed it on top of my carry-on. Just like in my dream, I was only taking a carry-on so I could skip the baggage check-in and carousel after the flight. I wanted to make this as simple and easy as possible.

I headed into the kitchen and grabbed a yogurt and banana, my breakfast on most days.

"Good morning, boys," I said to Josh and Greyson.

"Morning, Mom," they said as they shoveled cereal into their mouths, their eyes glued to the TV in front of them. I stood in the kitchen and started spooning the yogurt into my mouth. My eyes shifted over to the pile of bags by the door that Steve and the boys would be taking with them. We had packed everything last night so all Steve would need to do was get the boys from school, come home, and load up everything in the back of the car.

I stared at the duffel bags full of clothes, the boxes of food, the fishing gear, and all the other things they were taking. How many times had we packed up all this stuff to head to the cabin? I had never not gone with them. I could only remember one time when Greyson was really little and came down with a fever, and I sent Steve and

Josh ahead of us. Greyson and I joined them two days later when he was feeling better. I wouldn't be coming this time at all. Not only that, no one in my family knew where I was really going. I started getting this sick feeling in my stomach, and I couldn't even force the yogurt down, so I tossed it into the trash.

After breakfast began the mom-like organized chaos of getting everyone out the door. Steve was going to drop both boys off at school this morning since I had an early staff meeting. I made sure their backpacks were set to go and put their lunches inside. I helped Greyson tie his shoes and reminded Josh to turn in a field trip permission slip. It was time for me to leave, so I gathered my school bag and purse and went over to kiss the boys.

"Okay, guys. Mom's gotta go. Have a great time at the cabin and make sure to listen to Dad!" I said, giving Greyson a hug and kiss. I would have liked to give Josh a hug and kiss too, but he'd gotten away from that. "See ya on Monday, Josh," I said. I walked over to give Steve a kiss good-bye. "Bye, Steve. Have a great time and be careful," I said and without wanting to began to tear up. I hugged him and quickly tried to get rid of my tears.

"You okay, Reagan?" Steve asked.

"Oh, sure. I'm just going to miss you guys," I said, trying to keep my voice from wavering.

"Ha! You always wanted a break from us!" he said, hugging me back.

"Not really," I said.

"Well, have fun at your conference. I'm sure you and Kristen will have some adult beverages to make the time go faster," he said in a knowing voice.

"Probably a few," I said and winked at him.

"Okay, well, call me when you get to the cabin. You should be there well before I leave for the hotel," I told him.

"Will do. Bye," he said and walked into the living room where the boys were getting ready to go.

As soon as I got to work, Kristen rushed over to me immediately. "How are you doing, Reagan?"

"Well, let's just say if you had a valium handy right now, I wouldn't turn you down," I said.

"We just need to get through today and get you on that plane," she said, trying to comfort me.

"Yeah. Easy street from there," I said sarcastically. The morning went by uneventfully, and I got a text around 12:30 from Steve saying he had the boys and the car was packed. I texted back, *drive safe, luv u guys.* He sent back a thumbs-up and heart. Well, that's it. *They're off. I could still call this whole thing off,* I thought to myself. I would just drive up to the cabin in my car after work. That thought calmed me down, and then I got a text from Matthew.

All set? he sent.

Yep. Flight is at 7. I'll text you when I get to the hotel, I sent back.

Okay. Dad is doing really well.

Good to hear, I sent and put my phone away.

I had no idea how, but I made it through the afternoon. I walked the children out the door, and they all left, excited for the three-day weekend.

"Bye, Mrs. Bailey. Have a good weekend," Sienna said to me, giving me a hug and running off to her mom.

"I'll try," I said out loud to no one.

I went back to my room where Kristen found me and said, "5 o'clock?"

"Yep. See you then," I said and headed to the parking lot. I came home to an empty house, which was a very strange feeling. I could probably count on one hand how many times I had been in my house all by myself. I stared into the empty living room. There was no Greyson watching TV or Josh eating a snack. Steve was not outside mowing the lawn. Trixie wasn't even here to greet me. There was nothing. Silence.

I headed into my bedroom and finalized my packing. I checked my purse and made sure I had the cash I had pulled out of the ATM earlier in the week. My plane ticket was stashed in a zippered compartment. I checked the time on my phone: 4:45. Kristen would be here in fifteen minutes. I walked over to my hope chest and pulled out my mom's white shirt. I sat down on my bed, holding her shirt to my face and breathing deeply.

"What the hell am I doing, Mom?" I said out loud. I began to cry, and I wanted nothing more than to hear her voice say, "It's okay, Reagan."

I sat for a few minutes and then put the shirt back in the chest. I saw the letter from Jonathan. I picked it up and stared at my name on the envelope. I did not put it back in my hope chest. Instead I stashed it in the bag I was taking on the plane.

I heard a car horn and knew that Kristen had arrived and was in my driveway. I grabbed my bags and locked up the house. Kristen was in the driver's side on her phone, a familiar sight, which was comforting, considering I was about to do the most unfamiliar thing I had ever done. I placed my bags in the trunk and got in on the passenger side, and we began the twenty-minute ride to the airport. We chit-chatted about nothing all the way there, and I knew Kristen was trying to steady my nerves. It didn't work. We arrived at the airport terminal, and I got out and grabbed my bags.

Kristen gave me a hug, grabbed my hand, and said, "I hope you get the answers you are looking for, Reagan."

Me too. I reminded her that I'd text her when I arrived home on Monday and then ventured into the airport to find my gate number. I had flown on a plane before but never by myself. I stared up at the screens and found where I needed to go. It felt strange not to be checking in suitcases. It felt even stranger not to have my family with me.

I had at least an hour before I needed to board, so I decided to check out one of the airport bars. I ordered a glass of wine, hoping to calm my nerves down. My phone buzzed, and I looked down to see a text from Steve that read, *Made it safe and sound. Car is unpacked and boys are in the lake already.* I took a few sips of my wine and texted back, *Sounds great. We're heading to Illinois. I'll call you tonight.* He sent back a thumbs-up sign. I finished my wine and stared into my glass, thinking of my family up north. Why was I sitting in an airport bar instead of a lounge chair by the lake? The bartender came over and asked if I cared for another. *Sure, the whole bottle please. And one for the plane ride too.*

"No, thank you," I said. I got up and made my way over to my gate. I pulled out the magazine I had brought along and tried to flip through it, but my hands were shaking so bad that I couldn't even turn the pages. I put the magazine back in my bag, and I saw the letter from Jonathan. I pulled it out of the envelope and read it again. I read the last line over and over. *I'm loving you enough to let you go.* But did he have to let me go like that? I had cried myself to sleep for months after that, and it had taken every ounce of my being not to contact him. I didn't realize how much I would miss him until he was no longer in my life.

Eventually I moved on and met Steve and began my life with him, but there was a part of my heart that never fully healed. I put the letter back in my bag with the hope that I might get that healing now.

The flight attendant began calling for families to board. I almost jumped out of my seat and then realized I didn't have a family to board with. My seat number was in the middle of the plane, so I didn't have to wait too long to hear my row called. I stood in line and wondered who I would be sitting with. I handed my ticket to the attendant and then walked down the tunnel toward the plane. I found my seat, luckily a window seat, and I stored my bag above me. I sat down in my seat and waited for two passengers to join me. I really was in no mood for conversations, and I hoped my companions would be quiet.

After a few minutes, I was joined by a mother and her young son. Her husband and someone who appeared to be her daughter sat across from them. The boy had Mickey Mouse ears on and was bursting with excitement, as they were clearly on their way to Disney World. He sat in the middle, and the mother strapped him in. He looked about the same age as when we took Greyson for the first time, around four or so.

He looked over at me and said, "Hi! I'm Sam."

"Hi there. Are you on your way to Disney World?" I asked him.

"Yes! It's my first time going. Are you going to Disney World too?" he asked curiously.

"No," I said and winced inside waiting for the next question.

"Where ya going?" he asked.

Where *was* I going? I hesitated and said, "To see an old friend."

"How old?" he asked innocently. His mother interrupted then and apologized for his questions.

I reassured her that it was totally fine. "Well, he's not old like that. He's someone I haven't seen in a long time," I told my little friend.

"Why not?" he asked.

Hmmm . . . how should I answer that? "Well, he moved away and now he's kind of sick, so I'm going to visit him to make him feel better," was the best answer I could come up with.

"Oh. Where does he live?" he asked.

"Kind of by Disney World," I responded.

"You should go there with him. It might make him feel better," he said.

"Mmm . . . we'll see," I said.

Soon the flight attendant was going through instructions that I was not listening to. Hopefully the people around me would be able to save my ass, since I clearly would not know what to do. I heard the pilot say, "Prepare for takeoff," and I stared at the lighted seat belt sign above me. The plane began to move down the runway, and soon we were in the air. I couldn't contain my nerves and suddenly realized how tight my hands were clasped together. *Oh my God, I am actually flying to Florida*, I thought to myself, and I took some deep breaths, trying to calm down.

"First time flying?" my little buddy's mom asked me.

Although my nervousness was quite visible, she had no idea the reason behind it. *No, first time lying,* I wanted to say.

"No. I just don't care for it," I said and hoped there weren't more questions. She smiled and turned her attention to her son, and they started chatting about Disney. As I listened to their conversation, I couldn't help thinking I should be sitting next to Greyson discussing the new rides we wanted to try.

The pilot came on just then and welcomed us all as if it was his personal plane. He told us the current temperature in Florida and estimated arrival time. He told us to "settle in and enjoy the flight."

I stared out the window and wondered for the millionth time if I'd made the right decision. Questions began to flood through my brain like a tidal wave, and I couldn't stop it. *What if Jonathan relapsed and ended up in the hospital? What if one of my kids gets sick or hurt? What if Steve found out about this? What if Karen found out about this? Did I think this through enough?* I had no one there with me to help answer these questions. I was on my own. I put my thumb through my mom's ring and rubbed it back and forth with my finger.

The flight attendant began her trek down the middle aisle with the beverage cart. When she got to our row, I decided against any type of alcohol and asked for a white soda, hoping that would settle some of the nerves in my stomach. Sam ordered some juice and was fascinated by the little tray that folded down in front of him. He giggled as his juice was set down in front of him.

We both began to sip our beverages, and he turned to me again and asked, "What's your name?"

"Reagan," I answered.

"Do you have any kids?" he asked curiously.

"Yes. I actually have two little boys like you. Well, one is not so little."

"What are their names?" he asked.

"Josh and Greyson," I answered.

"Where are they?"

"They are up north with their dad. They're going camping this weekend," I said.

"Oh. Too bad you have to go see your sick friend," he said sipping on his juice.

"Well, that's okay. It will be summer pretty soon, and I'm a teacher and I'll have lots of time with them," I said, trying to make myself feel better again.

"You're a teacher?" his eyes widened. It's a familiar reaction, one I've seen many times when I run into one of my students at a store or restaurant.

"Yep. I teach kids a little bit older than you," I told him.

"I'm going to school next year," he said. His little red mustache melted my heart.

"Well, that will certainly be exciting," I said to him. He smiled.

The rest of the flight was uneventful, and soon enough the captain came on telling us to fasten belts and remain seated. The plane touched down, and that first bump shot through my body. We rolled to a stop, and he told us the temperature was around 78 degrees and the time was 10:15.

"Welcome to Florida," he said in a cheery voice. Well, I was here. Now what?

Chapter 20

I grabbed my bags, filed off the plane, and said good-bye to Sam and his family. I watched his little family of four scurry excitedly off to their adventure with talk of finding the Magical Express, and I felt a pang in my stomach and heart thinking of my family so far away. I stood in one place while people swarmed around me going in different directions but all with a definite place to go. I was frozen for a few seconds, and panic began to rise up and spread through my body. I took some deep breaths, trying to calm myself down.

Okay. I'd arrived. *Put the next step of the plan into place,* I told myself. I found the escalator that led to the exit where a lot of taxis were waiting. A man whose skin told me he'd spent many years in the Florida sun hailed a taxi for me, and I climbed in the backseat. I gave the driver the name of the hotel; he pulled away from the curb and started down the street. He tried to make polite conversation with me, asking if I was here for business.

"No," was all I said.

"Visiting someone, are you?" he asked again.

"Yes," I replied, hoping my one-word answers would deter him from asking more questions. It worked, and we drove in blessed silence. I pulled out my phone and texted Steve that I'd made it to Illinois and that Kristen and I were heading to get a drink. He texted back that the boys were asleep and to have a good time. I responded with *Okay. Call you tomorrow.*

The ride was about twenty minutes, and he was soon pulling

in front of the hotel. "Here you go," he said and offered a smile. I paid him the fare, adding a few bucks for tip, and vacated the taxi. I entered the hotel, and the first thing I noticed was a beautiful lobby with a gorgeous marble water fountain.

At the front desk, I was greeted by a young woman. "Welcome. Checking in?"

"Yes, the reservation is under Bailey," I told her and looked around nervously. It would be my luck that one of my students was heading to Florida for the weekend and staying at this very hotel.

"Yes. Mrs. Bailey, I see we have you for three nights." She handed me my key card with the room number and a map of the hotel. She explained on the map how to get to my room, and I seriously hoped my subconscious was listening, because I was sure the hell not. I felt a few small waves of panic thinking how Steve was the one who always did this part. I was seriously direction illiterate. I heard the words north or east and my brain literally shut down.

I grabbed the key card and map and started trying to figure out the way to my room. Somehow I managed to find it, room 304. I slid the key card in and waited for the light to turn green. I opened the door and entered the room, immediately noticing a nice, king-sized bed and a balcony. I pictured the boys running around the room and jumping on the bed as they usually did when we stayed at a hotel.

But the boys were not here. I was alone in Florida, and no one in my life except Kristen knew I was here. I sat down on the bed, and a single tear dripped down my cheek. Another tear followed, and soon tears were just streaming down my cheeks. I cried for how alone I was. I cried for the lies I had told my family. I cried for Jonathan and his impending death. I cried for the loss of my mom. I cried for my past, present, and future.

Then I called Matthew. He answered before the phone even had a chance to ring.

"Hello, Matthew," I said.

"Hello, Reagan. Are you here?" he asked with undeniable hope in his voice.

"I am," I said and felt myself trying to catch my breath.

"What's wrong, Reagan? Are you okay?" he asked.

"Yes. I'm just a little worn out. I'm sure I'll feel better once I get some sleep," I responded.

"Everything go okay with the flight and hotel?" he asked.

"Yep," was all I offered.

"Umm . . . so should we talk about tomorrow?" he asked in a cautious voice.

"Sure." I knew I should be offering more than one-word answers, but I was beyond the point of freaking out and moving well into the panic attack stage.

"Reagan, what's going on? Are you sure you're okay?" Matthew said in a very worried tone. I didn't say anything. I was afraid if I started talking, I would break down again, and I really didn't want to do that on the phone. "Would you like me to come there?" he asked.

"No. It's just . . . I'm so far away from my family, and they don't even know I'm here. I haven't seen your dad in twenty years. Twenty years! And now I'll be seeing him tomorrow only to say good-bye again. Well, actually to say good-bye for the first and last time. To be honest, I'm freaking out a little bit," I said.

"Well, of course you're freaking out, Reagan. Why wouldn't you be? How many times have you done this in your life? Never, right? So, you should be feeling all sorts of things. But don't mistake *this feels strange* for *I shouldn't have done this*," he said, trying to comfort me. It worked a little bit.

I collected myself and said, "Okay, what is the plan for tomorrow?"

"We are going to tell my mom that my dad and I are going to a golf outing at his country club," he said.

"Okay. Do you think she'll suspect anything?" I asked.

"No, I think it should be okay." Matthew continued, "I'll drive him over to your hotel around noon?"

"Okay. Tell him I'll be waiting by the fountain in the lobby," I told Matthew. Then I asked, "Matthew?"

"Yes?"

"Isn't he worried that someone will see us?"

"No. He's not. I think he's past the point of worrying about things," he said.

"Okay. I will see you tomorrow then?"

"Well, you'll see my dad. I won't be coming in," he said.

"Right. Well then, I'll see your dad tomorrow.

"Reagan?"

"Yes?"

"Thanks for coming."

I unpacked my things and hung up my clothes. I changed into shorts and a T-shirt and flopped on the bed with remote in hand. I flipped through the channels, not really watching anything at all. I was completely exhausted, both mentally and physically. I figured I would not be able to fall asleep, but within ten minutes, my eyes were closing. I fell into a deep sleep, hoping maybe this would be the night my mom came to me.

The next morning I blinked my eyes open, forgetting for a few minutes where I was. I heard the sound of the TV I had left on in the background. I checked my phone to see the time, which was 8:00. I lay in bed for a few minutes and thought about the day ahead. In four hours, I would see Jonathan. It was too early to call Steve, as it was only 7:00 back home, so I swung my legs out of bed and sat there, trying to decide what to do.

I suddenly realized how hungry I was, not having eaten much the day before. I looked over the hotel brochure and saw that there was a coffee shop by the lobby that was already open. I threw my hair back into a ponytail, slipped on my sandals, and took the elevator down to the first floor. I saw the sign "Coffee N' More" and walked over to check it out. There was a nice arrangement of baked goods displayed, tempting its visitors. I ordered a vanilla latte and a bagel with cream cheese and waited while the teenagers behind the counter made my breakfast. The young girl handed me my stuff and said, "Here you go, ma'am." *Ma'am.* I hated that. When the hell had I graduated from a Miss to a Ma'am?

The coffee shop had some cute little tables and chairs, so I sat at one and tried to eat my breakfast. I watched as people came and went, many of them tourists undoubtedly headed out for an adventurous day at one of the many theme parks. My adventure today was going to be quite different than theirs.

Two little girls in matching Minnie dresses came in with someone I assumed was their grandma. They each picked out a doughnut, chatting excitedly about the upcoming day. I tried not to stare at them, but I couldn't help myself. It was not only painful to see adult daughters out shopping with their moms, but seeing a grandma with her grandchildren was equally as painful. It was just another reminder of time lost. My nerves prevented me from finishing my food, so I just went back up to the room. I waited until about 9:00 to call Steve, hoping I wouldn't be waking anyone back home.

He answered on the third ring and said, "Hi, Reagan."

"Hi, how are you guys?" I said, hoping to make my voice sound as cheery as possible.

"Everything's going great. Boys are having fun, and Trixie is running around like a crazy person. Wait, someone wants to talk to you," he said, and I heard him hand off the phone.

"Hi, Mom!" said Greyson excitedly.

"Hi, honey! Are you having fun?" I asked.

"I caught a big fish this morning all by myself!"

"Oh wow! Tell Daddy to send me some pictures, okay?" I said, trying to keep my voice from wavering, and we continued to chitchat for a few minutes. My heart literally hurt talking to him so far away.

Steve got back on the phone just then and said, "So, how's it going?"

"Fine. We'll be heading over to the conference soon. We just got some breakfast," I lied into the phone, hating myself.

"Sounds good. We're going to spend the day fishing probably. Greyson and I are waiting for Josh to wake up," he said.

"Yeah, he does love to sleep in. The ride up went well? No problems?" I asked him.

"Yep. Ride was fine. How about you?" Steve returned the question.

"Drive here was fine . . . little bit of rush hour traffic getting here, but other than that, everything's going fine," I told him. *Yep, it's all good. Oh, and by the way, I am in freaking Florida!*

"I'm going to get some breakfast going for us, so how about I call you later?" he asked.

"Well, why don't I call you? I'm not sure what we'll all be doing today. I think I might be in this conference the majority of the day," I said to him.

"Okay, honey. Talk to you later. We love you," he said.

"Love you guys too," I said, and the call ended.

I sat on the edge of the bed, not quite believing I'd just had this conversation with Steve. Was this who I was? A liar? How in the world was that my mother's daughter? Well, I had come this far. I might as well try to figure it out.

I realized in a little under three hours, Jonathan would be here. I tried to keep calm, but I couldn't control the excitement that was building inside me. Was it okay to be excited? Shouldn't I be feeling worried, scared, ashamed?

I decided to push those negative feelings way down deep and focused on the anticipation of seeing him again. I should maybe prepare some type of conversation. What if we ran out of things to talk about? No, I didn't think I could prepare for something like this. I was just going to let things happen naturally. Even though I had plenty of time before he came, I started to lay out my clothes, jewelry, and makeup. It gave me something to do and kept my mind from going through every scenario possible. I took my new black dress off the hanger and held it out in front of me. I knew I shouldn't feel this way but I couldn't help the "first date" type of feeling that was coursing through my veins, making me feel as giddy as I had getting ready for the prom or something. I took a deep breath and went into the bathroom to start getting ready.

There was an awesome whirlpool tub that I filled to the brim and added plenty of bubble bath. I climbed in and sank all the way down until the bubbles touched my chin. *Holy cow!* This felt amazing. When was the last time I'd done something like this for myself? Try never. But that just comes with motherhood. My mother never went on spa days or weekend getaways. She was the most selfless person I ever knew. She considered cleaning the house or cooking a meal doing something for herself. I was quite certain that when my mom got to heaven, she had a broom in one hand and a soup pot in the other and, looking at God, said, "Where would you like me to start?"

I wished I had done more for her when she was alive to show her how much I appreciated her. I never felt like I did enough to save her. Should we have gone to a different doctor? Should we have tried Cancer Treatment Centers of America? Those commercials made me sick to my stomach. I turned them off every time they came on. I couldn't listen to stories about people on their deathbeds that were saved when I couldn't do that for my mom.

I reached down and scooped up a handful of bubbles. I blew them into the air and they fell towards the tub like little flakes of snow. I watched them swirl down and land on the other bubbles until they just became part of the mound. Same as snow. You can watch individual flakes falling in the sky, but you can't pick them out of a snow pile once they land.

I lay there thinking about that for a minute. Maybe that was the approach I needed to be taking. I needed to look at myself and all the things I had done in my life as the whole of who I was. My snow pile. This journey was just a part of who I was. Just one individual flake. That made me feel better as I stepped out of the tub and began to towel off. I'd gotten the snow figured out. Just needed the rose petals now.

Chapter 21

Jonathan woke up on the morning he was going to see Reagan with a sense of peacefulness. He got up late that morning and was relieved to see Karen already gone. He had encouraged her to spend the day with one of her friends shopping and going out to lunch. He knew they had decided to drive to this one shopping mall that was almost an hour away, so she wouldn't be in this area.

She had given up so much this last year to take care of him that he constantly felt guilty that she did nothing for herself. He just piled that on the guilt he already felt from his affair with Reagan and the fact that he was once again lying to Karen. He wondered how much guilt a heart could hold. Nevertheless, he was glad she would be gone when he went to see Reagan. He thought that it would be easier than facing her with this lie.

He had really started feeling pretty good again. Cancer tricked you that way, though. You could have a few good days where you feel pretty normal and you think the doctors must have gotten this wrong. Then something happens where you are slapped in the face with your reality again. He went into the kitchen and made himself some breakfast. He sat outside on the patio eating some toast and fruit. Matthew came out with shorts and wet hair, indicating he had just gotten out of the shower.

"So, today's it, Dad. What are you thinking about?" he asked.

"Well, I'm thinking about what to say to her. I've spent so much time thinking about finding her and getting her to come out here and arranging today that I didn't think about what would happen when I see her. To be honest, I'm nervous," Jonathan said.

Matthew said, "Well, Dad. Hopefully it will bring you some comfort that Reagan is probably feeling the same way."

"I guess so. I'm going to need to make a stop on the way, so we should leave fifteen minutes earlier," Jonathan said.

"Okay, where do you need to stop?" Matthew asked with a curious tone.

"A flower shop," he answered.

Jonathan finished his breakfast and went to take a shower. After, he stood looking in the mirror, wondering what Reagan would think of him now. His hair was grayer, and the cancer had taken a pretty decent toll on his body. He was thinner but not in good way. His eyes looked tired, defeated. If his charming good looks were what Reagan was looking forward to, she was sure to be disappointed.

"Hello, Reagan," he practiced saying in the mirror.

He got dressed and killed the rest of the time by watching some of the game on TV. Pretty soon it was time to leave. He grabbed the small, gold box he had purchased earlier in the week and told Matthew they should get going. They drove out of their neighborhood and headed in the direction of the hotel. Matthew searched for a flower shop on an app on his phone and found one not too far from where they were going. Matthew pulled into the parking lot, and Jonathan got out of the car. He walked in and searched around for the most beautiful rose he could find. He found one that had colors of red, orange, and yellow. He paid for the rose and then went to an area of the store, pulled off all the petals one by one, and piled them in the gold box. He shoved the box into his pocket and headed back out to the car.

"Where are the flowers, Dad?" Matthew asked him.

"I've got what I need," Jonathan said with a small smile on his face.

They continued to the hotel and were soon pulling into the circular driveway that led to the glass entrance door. Matthew pulled over and parked the car. Jonathan sat there, unable to move. They stayed in silence, each with their own thoughts about the encounter that was about to take place.

"Well, I guess I better go in, son," Jonathan said.

"I guess so. I hope you get what you came for, Dad," Matthew said, staring straight ahead.

"I can't thank you enough for all you have done for me. I would have never been able to do all of this without your help," Jonathan said and leaned over to hug his son.

Matthew half-heartedly returned the hug, and Jonathan understood why.

"Call me when you want me to pick you up," Matthew told him, and Jonathan nodded. He watched Matthew pull away until he was out of his sight. He stood there, hands in his pockets, staring up at the front of the hotel. Reagan was inside this building. *Well, this is it,* he said to himself, pulled open the heavy glass doors, and walked in.

He looked around the lobby area but did not see her anywhere. Although he didn't know what she looked like today, he had no doubt that he would recognize her. He wandered into this little coffee shop, but there was no one inside. He went into the bar and restaurant area, but there were only a few guys sitting at the bar having a liquid lunch. He walked back out of the restaurant toward the lobby and saw a woman in a black dress sitting by the fountain, her back to him. The woman had shoulder-length brown hair. He walked slowly toward her. She didn't hear him approaching.

"Reagan?" he asked softly. The woman turned around and stood up. It was her. Twenty years older but just as beautiful as he remembered. Her hair was shorter, little lines around her eyes, and a look of maturity that comes with age. She was not the young college girl holding textbooks under her arm. She looked like someone's wife, someone's mother, but there was no denying her beautiful hazel eyes. They could turn from greenish to brownish with just a hint of her smile.

"Jonathan?" she said, staring into his eyes. They stood staring at each other, not saying anything. Then she brought her hands up to cover her mouth and said, "Oh my God, Jonathan? Is it really you?" He nodded and reached out and touched her hair. He had always loved her hair. Last time he saw her, it was long and curly. She grabbed his hand and held onto it.

"Hello, Reagan," he said.

"Hello, Jonathan," she said back. He reached out and grabbed her, and they hugged tightly. They didn't let go for a long time, and it felt as if they were the only two people in the world. It was the same feeling he used to experience on their dates twenty years ago. When they pulled apart, he saw the tears in her eyes and knew she could see the same in his.

"Why don't we go for a walk," he said, grabbing her hand and leading her out of the building.

They headed toward the beach and found a path to walk on. It was silent at first, both of them figuring out what to say to each other. *What do I say to her?* Jonathan thought to himself. But he didn't have to worry, because Reagan took the lead and initiated the first words.

"It's been a long time," she said and smiled at him.

"Yes. That's for sure," he said and smiled back.

"Well, perhaps we should get to know each other again," she said.

"I think that's a good place to start," he said. So Reagan began chatting about starting her teaching career and meeting her husband through mutual friends. She talked about her two sons and their individual personalities. She talked about her dad a little bit and about her two brothers and how their lives turned out.

Then she began to talk about her mom and her cancer diagnosis. She didn't talk too much about her death, which Jonathan suspected was for his benefit. She also didn't talk about their relationship back then or the letter he'd left. It was surface-level talking, but at least it was a way to break the ice.

Then she said, "Now it's your turn." So Jonathan began talking about Matthew and his accomplishments and his family. He talked about finishing his career and moving to Florida for his retirement. He talked about the weather, golfing, and trips he took to Colorado. He didn't talk about Karen or the cancer.

They had walked quite a ways and Jonathan was winded from the walk, so she found a bench for them to sit on. They sat staring at the waves, each lost in the things they had said and the things they didn't say. He turned to look at her as she stared out at the ocean. He could not believe he was actually sitting next to her. He just wanted to touch her, make sure this was real and not a dream. And as if Reagan could read his mind, she reached over and placed her hand on his. They intertwined their fingers and continued to look at the ocean in front of them.

Finally Reagan broke the silence. "So, Jonathan," she said carefully, "Matthew has kept me informed about your cancer diagnosis. We don't have to talk about it, but I'm sure that's a big reason why I'm out here. I just want you to know how sorry I am. I know that doesn't help, but after going through what I went through with my mom, sometimes sorry is all there is to offer." Jonathan sighed. "Do you want to talk about it?" she asked.

"Not yet," he said.

"Well, if you remember, I'm a great listener," she said and bumped her shoulder into his.

"I remember lots of things," he said with a knowing smile.

"Me too," she said.

"What do you remember the most?" he asked curiously. She didn't answer at first, clearly thinking about her answer.

"I remember the way I felt about you," she said and looked straight into his eyes. "I have to ask you this, Jonathan, and I need you to be honest. Did you honestly love me, or was I your escape from reality?" She turned her eyes back to the ocean.

"Reagan, how could you even ask that? Of course I loved you. I loved everything about you. That's one of the reasons I wanted you to come out here. I wanted to make sure you knew that." He put his hands on her shoulders, forcing her to look at him. "I loved you, Reagan. And part of me still does. That doesn't all just go away because of the decisions we made."

"*You* made," she said.

"I made for both of us," he said back. She didn't say anything more about it, and the conversation got dropped. After a while, he asked, "Well, it's my turn. I have to ask you something, and I need you to be honest."

"Yes," she said and turned to look at him.

"Did you ever think of me in all these years?"

She smiled. "Of course I did, Jonathan. You were in my thoughts every day for a long time after we ended. Every time I would see rose petals or get caught in a rainstorm I would think of you. I would hear songs from back then, and I would instantly remember our time together. As the years went on, you became a part of the memories in my heart. I didn't think I would ever see you again, though."

She paused then asked, "And what about you? Did I ever cross your mind?"

"Reagan, you have crossed my mind so many times in the last twenty years that if I ever have to have a brain scan because of my cancer, the doctors will not find any tumors . . . they will find a million pictures of a beautiful woman with long brown hair and hazel eyes." Jonathan pulled her close to his side. She leaned her head on his shoulder, and they watched as the waves crashed against each other.

It was getting to be later in the afternoon, and he asked Reagan if she was hungry.

"I could eat something," she said.

So they ended up taking a taxi a little farther away to a quaint little restaurant. Jonathan had been there once and remembered how much he liked the atmosphere. They continued small conversation all the way there about things that had gone on in their lives the last twenty years. They arrived at the restaurant and got a little table outside that overlooked the ocean. Reagan ordered a glass of wine, but Jonathan stuck with water. His alcohol drinking days were over. They looked over the menu and each ordered a seafood dinner. He had not been out to eat in a long time. It felt so good to be doing something so normal, as abnormal as this situation was.

"So?" he said.

"So . . ." She looked at him.

"What do you remember most about your mom?" he asked.

She looked surprised at the question but didn't hesitate at all before answering, "Her generosity."

"Tell me about it," he said.

And with that statement, Reagan began to open up. "My mother was a very generous person, with her time, her advice, her gifts, her money. She gave and gave and never expected anything in return. She was genuinely happy for other people and never really expressed any type of jealousy. It really was something to admire, and I can only hope to be like that one day." Reagan hesitated, and Jonathan sensed she had more to say but was afraid to.

"What else, Reagan?" he asked.

"My mother was not a saint, she wasn't perfect. No one is. But when people die, other people put them up on a pedestal, only remembering them as these angels with no faults. My mom had faults, like anyone else. She was very opinionated at times and expressed those opinions regardless of how it came across. She could be controlling at times too." Jonathan could sense that Reagan was glad to get that off her chest. "I've never spoken that way about her to anyone," she said with shame in her voice.

"I think it's good to remember all of it . . . it helps you keep things in perspective," he offered.

"I guess," she said.

Jonathan knew the answer to his next question might be hard for him to hear, but he really wanted to know. "Was she scared?" he asked and looked out the window.

"What do you mean?"

"At the end, did she seem scared to die?"

"You know, she never really said she was scared or showed it to us. If it were me, I think I would just be freaking out, worrying about everything I was leaving behind. In the last month of her life, she knew she was dying. She told me she could feel something changing in her body. But she didn't really seem worried or scared about it. I would bring up things like how I was too young to lose my mom, and she would respond with something like, *I can't do anything to change it.* I think something must happen to you in those last stages of your life."

"How so?" Jonathan asked her.

"I just don't think you have room in your mind to worry about all the things everyone around you is worrying about. You only have room to reflect on your life and the new journey you're about to face. Otherwise, I think people would die from sheer panic other than the cancer." She paused and then said, "That's my theory." She placed her hand on top of Jonathan's and offered a comforting smile.

The waiter appeared just then, breaking the heavy conversation, and set down their platters in front of them. Reagan had ordered a shrimp pasta dish, and he watched as she began to eat. He started to eat his food too and was suddenly blessed with a great appetite. Reagan shifted the conversation to something lighter, and they ate and talked and laughed and remembered. Things were going exactly as he pictured, and he felt so relieved and happy.

After they finished eating, they went to the bar and Reagan ordered another glass of wine and Jonathan ordered a club soda. They continued reminiscing and talked late into the afternoon. Jonathan knew he would have to get home soon or Karen would be worried. They took a taxi back to the hotel and got out and walked to the beachfront, again staring at the waves. The temperature was dropping, and the air felt a little cooler. They sat on the edge of the sand; Reagan kicked off her sandals and put her feet in the water. Jonathan sat with his legs out in front of him, watching the waves crash against each other. He grabbed a handful of sand and let it sift through his fingers. He knew he needed to start the inevitable conversation that was coming.

"I want to talk to you about my letter, Reagan."

She didn't say anything.

"I had to let you go. I knew I could never leave Matthew, and Karen didn't deserve what I was doing to her."

She still didn't say anything.

"But just because I ended things, it doesn't change the fact that I loved you. I don't know how it's possible to love two people at the same time, but it just is. I never felt about anyone the way I felt about you."

"Why am I here, Jonathan? Why did you ask me to come out here?" Reagan asked him.

"Because I'm going to die. And when you are facing the end of your life, it forces you to look back at all the things you did and didn't do. I knew how much that letter was going to hurt you, but I also knew if I talked to you in person, I wouldn't be able to do it. I was selfish that way," he said, hoping to make her understand. He watched as her eyes filled up with tears.

"Do you have any idea how much I loved you, Jonathan? Do you have any idea what finding that Dear John letter did to me?" she said angrily. She stood up and faced the ocean with her arms crossed.

Jonathan got up and stood next to her for a few moments, watching the silent tears drip down her face. "I'm sorry, Reagan."

"When Matthew first called me, I told him I wasn't going to come. Did you know that? I thought about sending *you* a letter this time."

"What changed your mind?" he asked.

"I found something. Something that my mom wrote and never shared with me. I felt like she was telling me to do this." She turned to him with eyes blazing. "After all that we meant to each other, I had to come to work and find a fucking Dear John letter. You broke my heart. I never got a chance to say good-bye, and now you're having me come out here for what? I lied to my husband, my kids. Do you realize that?"

"Yes, I realize that. I lied to my wife too. AGAIN!" Jonathan said forcefully.

"You son of a bitch. Are you really going to throw that in my face right now? You were an adult back then, and you're an adult now. You made choices, and I never forced you into anything," Reagan said. Jonathan saw her whole face start to quiver.

"I'm sorry, Reagan. I didn't mean that the way it sounded."

"And now I came out here only to lose you all over again." She put her hands in her face and began sobbing.

"You meant everything to me. Please believe me," he said quietly.

"I don't know how to believe you. You never gave me a chance to say good-bye. You took that moment from me. This is all I had to remember you by. I didn't even have a damn picture of you." With that, she whipped an envelope from her bag and threw it at him and started walking back to the hotel.

"Reagan! Don't go. Please, Reagan!"

She didn't stop, and pretty soon he couldn't see her anymore. Jonathan knelt down and picked up the envelope and saw his writing on the front. He sat back down at the edge of the sand and opened it up. He began to read his words from twenty years ago. He couldn't believe she'd kept this letter all these years. He put his face in his hands and broke down crying, not sure what to do.

After a while, he called Matthew to pick him up. He walked a little along the shoreline while waiting for him to come. He noticed a sailboat far onto the horizon and watched until he could no longer see it. "There she goes," he said to himself as he saw Matthew's car pull into the hotel parking lot. He threw a few shells in the water and headed over to the car.

Chapter 22

I quickly walked through the lobby and headed to the elevator, pressing the up button as hard as I could. I looked up, watching the elevator numbers trickle down from the floors above. Finally the doors opened, and I stepped inside, pressing 3 and willing the doors to shut quickly. I was literally shaking from head to toe and crossed my arms and pressed them to my body as tight as I could.

My phone buzzed. I looked at the screen and saw that Steve was calling. There was no way I could talk to him right now, so I let it go to voice mail. The elevator stopped, and I got off and made my way to my hotel room. The sound of the door locking behind me made me feel safe. Why the hell had I put myself on this journey? I lay down on the bed and cried silently into the pillow.

I must have fallen asleep, because an hour later I heard a knocking at my door. I walked over to the door, opened it, and found myself staring into the same denim-blue eyes of the man I loved so many years ago. But these eyes did not belong to Jonathan.

"You must be Matthew," I said, leaning against the opened door.

"Hello, Reagan," he said in the same tone of voice as his father's. "Can I talk to you?" he asked.

"Sure," I responded, and we both just stood there. I realized I must look like an awful mess, so I asked him to meet me in the hotel bar in ten minutes. I changed out of my black dress, which was wrinkled by now, and pulled on jeans and a tank top. I pulled my hair into a ponytail and fixed my makeup. I stared at the elevator floor all the way down to the lobby, not knowing what to do. I saw Matthew sitting at the bar drinking a beer and sat down next to him. I had no idea what to say.

"Can I get you a drink?" he asked.

"Sure. I'll take a brandy and Coke," I said. The bartender handed me the glass and I took a long drink, telling myself not to chug the whole thing down.

"Well, my father was right," he said.

"About what?"

"You really are very beautiful," he said. I half-smiled, still not knowing how to take a compliment.

"What did he tell you about today?" I asked.

"He said you had a nice day reminiscing and getting reacquainted. He said you became upset when talking about how the relationship ended, and he didn't know what to do," Matthew said pretty matter-of-factly and drained his glass. He motioned the bartender for another.

"Yeah. I did. I'm sorry if I upset him, but I didn't realize how I was going to react to the conversation until it was too late. Is he okay?" I asked.

"Yeah. He's okay. He's home and resting. He was a little worn out," Matthew said.

"I didn't mean to cause a problem. I know he wanted me to come out here so he could make amends before he dies. I came out here to get closure. I'm just not sure I'm going to get it," I said.

"Why not?"

"Well, closure means putting an end to something. I never wanted us to end," I said, realizing it for the first time. "I loved your dad, Matthew, and part of me always will. I don't feel bad about it or ashamed. It was real . . . as real as any love between two people. I never loved anyone the way I did Jonathan, including my husband, who I love very much. Just like I have never loved anyone the way I love my husband. And I think that's okay. Every relationship has a unique love story."

"I'm sorry for any hurt I caused you in coming out here, Reagan. I was just trying to do right by my dad," Matthew said.

"I know, Matthew. I'm an adult, and I made a choice to come here. No one forced me," I said.

"Do you know what made me come out here, Matthew?" I asked him. I had never told him about the note I found in the book.

Matthew shook his head while putting another dent in the liquid in his glass.

"I found something. Something my mom wrote but never showed me."

"What did it say?"

"Well, she told me I shouldn't leave this world with any regrets. And I knew if I didn't make this trip out here, I would regret it for the rest of my life. So no matter what the consequences of this trip are, I will never be sorry I came to see Jonathan."

"And I will never be sorry I asked you to come," Matthew said. "Well, I'd better get going." He threw some money on the bar and stood up to leave.

I looked down into my glass and said, "What about tomorrow, Matthew?"

"I'll be in touch," he said. He started to leave and then turned back around and set a small gold box on top of the bar. "He said to give you this." And with that, Matthew walked out of the hotel.

I stared at the gold box and played with the ribbon on top for a long time. I grabbed the box and headed out to the beachfront. By now, it was dark and the moon was shining bright above the ocean waters. The wind was blowing a gentle breeze—it was a beautiful, still night. I glanced down the pathway where Jonathan and I had walked mere hours before. I now had a new memory to file in with all the old ones of Jonathan and me. I never thought that would happen.

I sat down cross-legged and set the gold box in my lap. I knew what was inside. I didn't need to open it. All of a sudden, I felt a presence next to me, and the hairs on the back of my neck stood up. I knew my mom was there, surrounding me, trying to comfort me, to once again take care of me.

"Hi, Mom," I said out loud. I began telling her about my trip and my encounter with Jonathan. I would pause sometimes, imagining what she would say to me. It was as close as a two-sided conversation I was ever going to get with her again. "Do you know what's in this box, Mom? This is Jonathan's way of making me remember."

It's my way too, I could literally hear her say as if she were sitting next to me speaking out loud. All of a sudden, a feeling went through me that I couldn't describe even if I had all the words in the world to choose from. Jonathan had delivered to me what my mom could not. She was coming through on my request . . . rose petals in unexpected places. And this situation was about as unexpected as it could get.

I was still sitting by the ocean staring up at the bright moon when I heard my phone buzz. I looked down to see a text from Matthew. I looked closer and saw the words were actually from Jonathan. I read it and felt a sense of relief that I would be seeing him tomorrow. I looked at his words and hoped that he could come through on what he was saying. I grabbed the gold box and walked down the path toward the hotel to call Steve.

Chapter 23

Well, now what? Jonathan thought to himself. He had been sitting on the patio for over an hour staring at the moon. He had absolutely no fucking clue what to do. He was not surprised that Reagan got so angry. She'd been holding it in for over twenty years. The patio door opened, and Matthew came out.

"Hey, Dad. How are you doing?"

"Okay." He put his hands behind his head and stared at Matthew. "Did you talk to her?" he asked, raising his eyebrows.

"Yes."

"What did she say?" he asked, staring at his son. "You've been gone for a while." A wave of unbelievable jealousy washed over Jonathan, thinking of Reagan and Matthew having some intimate conversation. He knew that wasn't fair, but when you're dying, all fairness goes out the window.

"She says she is sorry she upset you and she didn't mean to cause any problems."

"Is that all?"

"No. She also said she loved you and she doesn't think she can get the closure she needs."

Jonathan thought about that for a moment. "Well, I need to fix this. I'm running out of time." *Not just this weekend but in my life,* he thought.

"What do you want to do?" Matthew asked.

"Give me your phone," Jonathan said. He went to Matthew's

messages and texted Reagan. He handed the phone back to Matthew. "Goodnight, son," Jonathan told Matthew and headed inside to go to bed.

Matthew looked down at the text and saw what his dad had sent Reagan.

Reagan, You've come a long way to not get closure. I couldn't give you back then what you needed, but I hope I can give you what you need now. Meet me in the lobby at noon. Me

Chapter 24

I woke up the next morning and went for a long walk on the beach. It was not the typical sunny day in Florida like we had yesterday—gray and cloudy but no raindrops yet. I dressed a little more casually this time and waited by the fountain for Jonathan. I didn't know how he was going to explain another day away from home to Karen, but I couldn't worry about it. That was his problem to solve. I saw him walk in, and he came over to me.

"Hello, Reagan," he said and held out his hand.

"Hello, Jonathan," I grabbed his hand and we stood up.

"I brought my car so we can drive somewhere," he said.

"Are you sure you feel like driving?" I asked. I knew that my mom pretty much gave up driving in her last few months.

"Yes. It makes me feel normal."

"Okay, where do you want to go?" I asked.

"I want to take you somewhere," he said and opened the car door for me. We drove for a little bit; there was no conversation between us. I had no idea where he was taking me. The drive was short, and soon he was pulling into what looked like a park. I read a sign that said *Babe Ruth Youth Baseball Stadium*.

"What are we doing here?" I asked. Jonathan didn't answer. He pulled into a parking space and parked the car. I watched as he got out and came around to my side. He opened my door and reached for my hand.

"Come on," he demanded. I walked with him into the stadium

and followed him toward the fan bleachers. He began to climb up them and led us to an open section, where we sat for a while.

"You want to watch a baseball game?" I asked.

He watched the game for a little bit. I was not sure what the hell this was about.

"Jonathan, why are we at a high school baseball game?"

He continued watching the boys play, and without turning to look at me, he began to talk.

"Twenty years ago, I was sitting at a baseball game just like this, watching Matthew play for his high school team. All of a sudden, he took a ball to the head and fell to the ground. He was knocked out for a few moments. Karen and I rushed him to the hospital and had to wonder if something serious was wrong. It turned out okay, but watching him lie there in that hospital bed, so young and so vulnerable, I knew I could never leave him. I wouldn't just be leaving Karen, but I would be leaving my son behind. That would have broken his heart. And as much as I loved you, I would never do anything to hurt my son. And you wouldn't have been able to understand it because you weren't a mother. But now you are. So I want you to look out at those boys out there and picture Josh and Greyson's faces. Now picture what you splitting up your family would do to them."

My eyes filled with tears, and I let them fall without bothering to wipe them away. Jonathan reached for my hand, and we sat like that, watching the game, both us of thinking how all of our lives would have turned out if Jonathan had not walked away.

We returned back to the hotel as raindrops started to appear on the windshield. He pulled in front of the lobby and put the car in park. We both got out, and he walked me into the hotel. We stood by the fountain, silent . . . not knowing how to end. We both started talking at the same time.

"Reagan, I—"

"Jonathan—"

We laughed and finally he said, "Reagan, you have made my final wish come true even though I probably didn't deserve it."

"You have helped me too, Jonathan, and I am so glad I came."

"Here. I thought you might want this back," he said and handed me the envelope with my name on it. I took it and placed it in my bag.

We stood staring at each other until once again I broke the silence by saying, "Well, I'd better let you get back home."

"Yeah," he said quietly, staring at the floor. I reached for his hand and smiled at him.

"Good-bye, Jonathan."

"Good-bye, Reagan."

We hugged for a few moments and slowly pulled apart. I let him go and watched him walk out to his car. I began walking toward the elevators and pressed the up button. My mind and heart were racing—I couldn't let him go yet.

I ran back outside. It was pouring rain, but I didn't care. I ran toward his car. He looked up, saw me, and he jumped out of the car. I ran toward him and jumped in his open arms. He grabbed my face and pulled me to his face. My mouth found his, and we shared a kiss that transported me to the back hallway of a little bar that I couldn't remember the name of, but began this journey with Jonathan. The rain poured on us and around us, but neither of us let go. Finally we pulled apart and stared into each other's eyes.

"I love you, Reagan. I always have," he said, and I heard the emotion in his voice.

"I love you too, Jonathan."

We embraced again, and I laid my head on his shoulder and tried to breathe in my last moment on Earth with him. Finally we pulled apart. He cupped my face in his hands and gave me one last kiss . . . a kiss good-bye.

He opened the car door, but before he stepped in, he turned to me and with his signature smile said, "We make good memories in the rain."

I smiled at him and watched him drive away. It was over.

I headed upstairs to my room, dried off, and went out on the balcony that overlooked the ocean. I watched the rain bouncing off the waves and thought about the night my mom died. After my dad and brothers returned to the hospice facility, we all stood around my mom's bed looking down at her body. The original five now down to four.

My dad looked like his heart had been ripped in two. He sat in a chair next to her with his hand placed on hers. The hand he had held his whole life. He spoke to her in a voice so softly that no one could hear what he was saying. I have never asked him to this day what he said to her in that moment. It was a moment their entire marriage had led to. My brothers were silent, wiping away tears as they tried to process the fact that their mother was gone. I remembered thinking that the glue that held our family together was no longer here. We would have to move forward on our own. How would we do that? Could I fill that role?

Over the past year and a half, our bond continued to remain solid and strong because of everything she taught us about family, love, compassion, generosity, and strength. I knew I could never fill her role completely but the parts of me that came from her would sure as hell try.

About an hour later, I heard a familiar knock on the door. I knew who it was before I even opened it. "Lead the way," I said as I opened the door. Matthew smiled and nodded, and we headed toward the elevator. Neither of us said anything on the ride down, each lost in our own thoughts. We sat down in our same seats at the bar and ordered the same drinks again.

"Well, we have to stop meeting like this," Matthew said, and we both laughed. We sipped our drinks, and Matthew finally said, "Tell me, Reagan."

"Tell you what?"

"Tell me what the end is going to be like. I need to know," he said and looked at me.

"Well, I'm sure it's different for every person," I said.

"Death is death. What am I in for?" he half smiled, but I knew . . . I remembered the anticipation of the actual moment.

"Well, the very last day, my mom was very unresponsive. She just lay there but did not talk or move or reach for me. She breathed in and out of her mouth but never stirred. I touched her all day long, but she felt different. I wanted only for her to grab my hand or hold her arms out to me, but that never came. I sat by her side, and I knew this was going to be it. The nurses said a few more days possibly, but to me she was already gone. She had entered her new life, and just her physical body lay there.

That night, the nurse went to check her, and her pulse had stopped. I stood in shock for few moments because I could not believe this was it. The nurse reminded me to grab her hand and talk to her. And so I did. I held her hand, and then I hugged her body to mine and said over and over, "I'm going to miss you, Mom." I laid her back on the pillow, and that was it. There was no noise, no final gasp of breath, nothing. She was gone. My mom was dead."

"Jesus, Reagan. I'm so sorry for you too. How do you feel now that some time has gone by?" I knew he was asking for himself. He wanted to know how he was going to deal with all of this, but I had to be honest.

"Well, Matthew. I'll tell you how I feel now that she's been gone a while. I feel cheated. You know in your teens, you are too cool for your parents. You are embarrassed by pretty much everything they do. In your twenties, you are too smart for them. You know everything about everything and think you've got the world by the ass. In your thirties, you are too busy for your parents with your career, marriage, and raising babies. In your forties, you are still busy but your career is established and your kids are getting older and more independent, and now you have time to really appreciate your parents and be there for them and spend more time with them. I got cheated out of the chance to truly appreciate her."

Matthew did not say anything. I knew he was thinking about what I had just said and realizing that he would be cheated too. I did not want to make him feel worse than he already did, but I needed to tell him how I felt. And in some ways, talking with Matthew, I was discovering for the first time how I *really* felt.

I placed my hand on top of his and said, "Matthew, you are about to join a club that absolutely no one wants to be a part of. And the shitty part is you can't return the unwanted membership. But I can tell you that each day it gets a little easier. I used to wake up every morning after her death with this desperate feeling of having a problem that will never be solved. But then, there came a time when it was not the first thing I thought of. It would creep in my mind later in the day at some point. And then there were some days that I didn't think about it at all. Then I got to feel guilty for not thinking of her. And you never know what will trigger sadness or when it will come. I think some of the hardest times for me are at night when it is quiet, dinner is done, the boys are playing, and I think this would be a good time to call her. And then I remember that I can't all over again."

Matthew kind of nodded, and I could tell he was just taking in everything I was saying.

"You know, Matthew, part of me wanted to come out here just

so I could tell you that despite all the heartache you're about to face, you will get through this and come out somewhat okay on the other side," I said, squeezing his hand before letting go.

There was something else I wanted to tell him . . . a conversation I had been avoiding. I looked at him and then looked down at my drink. I looked at him again and again looked away.

"What is it, Reagan?" Matthew asked, sensing my hesitance.

"Well, I really don't know quite how to bring this up," I said.

"Reagan, you flew part way across the country to see my dying father, and there are only a few people in the whole world who know that, you and I being two of those people. I don't think there's much you can't say to me. What is it?" he said and grabbed my seat, turning it toward him.

"Well, it's about back then," I said and began to play with my mother's ring.

"Yeah. What about it?"

"Well, I guess I want to explain how this all happened . . . maybe even apologize for it," I said to him.

"Look, you really don't owe me a explanation. It was a long time ago," he said.

"Well, you must be wondering how . . ." I paused, embarrassed, not knowing how to say the next few words.

"How he could do this to my mom?" Matthew finished the sentence for me.

I shrugged my shoulders and looked at his face. "Well, don't you want to know our story?"

"Not really."

"Oh," I said in a tone that indicated he'd gotten his point across. He was not interested in our story.

"Well, if you could tell me one thing about it, the most important thing, what would you say?" Matthew asked me.

"I'd tell you that we fought against it until we couldn't any longer. And I probably should apologize for what we did, but there was no way it was not going to happen. It was the strongest connection I have ever felt with anyone in my entire life."

We finished our drinks, stood up, and faced each other.

"Well, Matthew, I better let you get back," I told him.

"Reagan, I don't even know where to begin in saying thank you," Matthew said, and I saw the tears in his eyes.

"I should thank you. I needed to do this."

"Good-bye, Reagan. Take care of yourself," Matthew said and held out his hand to shake mine.

I grabbed his hand and pulled him to me. We hugged, and I whispered, "Hold him when he goes, Matthew. It will be something you can carry with you." I walked out of the bar and headed up to my room. My journey was almost over. I just had one more thing I wanted to do.

The next morning, I woke up early, packed up all of my things, and checked out of the room. I left my bags at the front desk and walked out to the ocean. I stood hugging my arms to my body, staring out at the water, watching the waves move back and forth.

I looked down the shoreline and once again pictured Jonathan and me walking along the sand. I tried to burn that image in my brain. I slowly breathed in and out as the warm, salty air filled my lungs. After some time, I pulled out the small gold box I had tucked in the pocket of my shirt. I pulled at the ribbon and took the cover off. There, nestled on some white fluffy tissue, was a pile of colorful rose petals. I touched them and let them sift through my fingers.

Like petals in the snow. I smiled to myself.

I knelt down and found the place where the water met the sand. I tossed the petals into the water and watched as the waves slowly carried them away. There was a yellow petal that shone brightly among all the others . . . almost winking at me. "Good-bye, Jonathan," I said to the petals, to the ocean, to my journey out here.

I watched until I could no longer see the them. I stood up and walked back to the hotel to get a taxi to the airport. I was ready to go home.

Chapter 25

I stood on the sidewalk in front of the glass entrance doors to my airline waiting for Kristen to come. I held my bag in my hand and my heart in my throat. In the past seventy-two hours, I felt like I lived my past, present, and future. The flight home had been less eventful than on the way there. I sat next to an older man who spent the entire flight reading. I glanced at the title of the book he was so engrossed in—it was called *What Questions Haven't I Asked You?*

Well, that's certainly a book I could have written. I whipped out a paper and pen and spent a good part of the flight writing down all the things that had been circling my mind and heart for the past year and a half.

Pretty soon Kristen's Ford Explorer turned the corner, and I stepped out on the curb, anxious to separate myself from the airport. I threw my bag in her backseat and climbed in the front.

"All set?" she asked.

"Yep," I said, and she pulled away from the curb and started on the route to my house. She didn't say anything. I figured she was waiting for me to start pouring my heart out, as I had done with her so many times over the past twenty years. But I didn't do that. There was no accurate way to explain what I had just experienced, so I didn't even want to try.

Finally, she simply asked, "How did everything go?"

I had texted her a little bit throughout the weekend just to let her know I'd arrived okay and had connected with Jonathan and all was well.

"Well, I am glad I went, and I'm glad I'm home," I told her. I wasn't ready to share the details yet; she understood and didn't press for any. I knew someday I would be able to share more with her.

We arrived at my house, and I thanked her for everything.

"You're welcome, Reagan. See you tomorrow," she said and pulled out of the driveway.

It was early afternoon, and Steve and the boys had not arrived home yet. He had texted me earlier that they would be home closer to dinnertime. I was glad to arrive home first and get settled. As I began unpacking my bag, I pulled out the envelope from Jonathan. Inside was the letter that ended our relationship. I walked over to my hope chest and set it inside. I closed the lid on the hope chest and my past.

I finished unpacking, took a quick shower, and was sitting on the patio in the backyard when I heard Steve's car pull up.

Greyson's voiced echoed through the house. "Mom? Mom?"

"I'm out on the patio, buddy!"

He ran to me and gave me the biggest hug. "Hi, Mom!"

"Hi, honey! How are you?" I hugged and kissed him.

"Good! I caught so many fish!" he exclaimed excitedly.

"I know! Daddy sent me all the pictures!"

"How was your trip?" he asked me.

"Oh, just fine. But I sure missed you guys," I said.

"I missed you too!" he said and gave me another hug.

Steve and Josh came out the patio door with Trixie. She jumped on my lap and started kissing my face.

"Hi, guys," I said to Steve and Josh.

"Hi, Reagan," Steve said, giving me a kiss and hug.

"Hi, Mom," Josh said and gave me a half hug. I knew he was trying to act too cool to show that he missed me, but I knew he did.

We sat around the patio talking about the weekend. I heard lots of fishing stories and one story about a possible bear sighting that was never confirmed. The boys told me about some interesting dinners over the campfire, boat rides, and swimming in the lake.

"Well, it sure sounds like I missed a great time!" I said and felt a pang in my heart.

"That's okay, Mom! We'll go lots more this summer," Greyson said. He was the one who always tried to make everything better.

"How did everything go at the conference?" Steve asked.

"Oh, fine. We got a lot of information to bring back to school," I said. I really wanted to end this whole lying business, so I hoped he wouldn't ask too many questions.

"So, what does everyone want for dinner?" I asked, and with that question, everyone began talking at once. We all headed into the house to start unpacking and make dinner plans.

Later that night, after the boys were in bed, Steve and I hung out together, watching TV and talking about the weekend.

"So was it just all meetings and lectures the whole time?" Steve asked innocently.

"Umm, yeah. Pretty much," I said, trying to sound believable.

"Did you guys get any time to go out?" he asked.

"Yeah. Not too much, but we managed to sneak a few glasses of wine in here and there," I said. *How much longer was this conversation going to last?*

"So are you glad you went?" he asked, not realizing how much meaning was behind that question.

I didn't respond right away.

"Reagan? Did you hear me? Are you glad you went?" he said, looking at me curiously.

I looked straight at him. "Yes. I am."

"Well that's good, considering you had to give up a whole weekend for this," he replied.

We continued watching TV for a few minutes.

"Steve?"

"Yeah?" he replied, not taking his eyes off the screen.

"Although I learned a lot of things this weekend, I really learned how much I love you and the boys. I missed you guys like crazy," I said and reached over to hug him.

He seemed a little surprised at that reaction. "We missed you too, Mama," he said.

I fell asleep on the couch that night, lying in Steve's arms. I didn't dream of my mom or Jonathan. I didn't dream of roses, airports, or old letters. I didn't dream at all. I slept a peaceful, uninterrupted sleep lying in the arms of my husband. I was home.

A few days later I found myself standing in front of my mother's crypt, staring at the engraved lettering.

"Well, Mom, I did it. I went to Florida to see Jonathan. Your spirit guided me every step of the way. I know you were there with me, Mom. I felt you on the beach. I learned a lot about myself on this trip, and I'm glad I got the chance to say good-bye to him. In some ways, I felt like I was finally saying good-bye to you." I pulled out the paper I had written on the plane.

"I wrote something, Mom. I wrote down all the questions I've wanted answers to since you died." I began to read out loud the questions on my paper. Questions that ranged from *Did you hear me in the last moments before you died?* to *Where is the recipe for the hot bacon dressing?* Questions that I would never get answers to. I continued reading until I got through every question on my paper.

When I finished, I folded the paper neatly and placed it in the crack between her crypt and the next one. I traced the letters of her name and pressed my forehead to the cold, hard metal. The image of her holding her arms out to me for one final hug flooded into my brain. I dropped to the sidewalk below, covered my face with my hands, and broke down. I looked up at her crypt and through uncontrollable sobs said out loud, "I just wish I could talk to you one more time." After some time, I stood up and wiped my eyes.

"Your last wish was for me to know how strong I am. But when you were alive, you were the one who gave me strength. And now you're gone. So I had to learn to be strong for Dad, the kids, the family. I have had to be strong for me too. I had to keep going on days that I just wanted to crawl under a blanket. I had to put my own grief aside to help everyone else get through this. I had to stare down at you lying in that coffin with that awful pink lipstick they put on you and tell myself that this was for the best . . . that you were out of pain."

"And I've learned how to do it . . . to be strong. Because I am your daughter." Maybe I wouldn't get any rose petals in front of my house during a winter snowstorm, but I was doing what she would have wanted me to do.

∾ ∾ ∾

After I left the cemetery, I stopped by my dad's house. He was sitting outside with a cup of coffee and the newspaper.

"Hi, Reagan." He stood up and gave me his usual hug. "How was your trip?"

"It was fine. I was glad to come home. I have something to show you," I told him, sitting down at the patio table.

"What?"

"Do you remember that book I took a few weeks ago? From Mom's shelf?" *God, was that really only a few weeks ago that I found that note?* "Yes."

"Well, I took it on my trip, and I found something inside the book," I told him.

"What did you find?" he asked.

I pulled out the note my mom had written. The note that was titled *My Last Wishes.*

The note that prompted me to go on this journey. I slid it across the table toward him.

"What is this?"

"Just read it," I said, and I watched as my dad unfolded the paper and saw her handwriting. I heard his gasp as he began to read. He read it slowly and carefully and then pulled a handkerchief out of his pocket and wiped his eyes.

"So you didn't know about this?" I asked him.

"No. I've never seen it," he said.

"When do you think she wrote this?" I asked.

He paused, looking out at the unplanted garden, and then said, "When she knew."

I nodded and said, "Well, you keep it, Dad. You can show this to the rest of the family some time."

"Don't you want it?" he asked.

"No. I want you to have it. I want you to read it every day and think about her words. You still have a lot of life to live, Dad, and you have all of us," I said.

"I know, but that life without your mother is not a life I ever wanted," he said and continued to let the tears flow.

"No one wanted this, Dad. No one expected this or deserved this. But it happened. She's gone. We can't change it, but we can learn to accept it," I said and placed my hand on top of his.

He glanced at the paper again and said, "But Reagan, maybe you want to hang onto this so you can read her words."

"That's okay, Dad. I already know what she wanted for me," I told him.

We sat outside for a while, and then my dad turned to me and asked, "So, what should we do about the garden?"

"Let's go check it out," I told him, and we stood up and walked over to the back of the yard, arm in arm.

Chapter 26

Our daily lives continued. I finished the school year, and summer began. It was the middle of June when I received a text from Matthew. *Reagan, my dad has taken a turn for the worse and will be entering hospice in the next few days.* I texted back, *Stay strong for him, Matthew.*

I did not hear from Matthew again for a few weeks. On the fourth of July, I was sitting on a blanket, surrounded by my family, watching the colorful explosions in the night sky. I felt my phone vibrate, indicating a text. I glanced at the screen and saw there was a message from Matthew. I couldn't read it just then, but I knew what it said. My heart dropped, and I was just trying to breathe. I stared into the night sky, and off to the side of the fireworks, I saw two bright lights. I saw Josh look over at them too; he turned to me and said, "What are those, Mom?"

"I'm not sure, honey, stars?" I said. But in my head I said, *Mom, meet Jonathan.*

We finished watching the fireworks, and the oohs and aahs became louder as the finale began. I stared into that July sky and searched not for stars and planets, but for peace to finally fill my heart.

We drove home, and Steve asked, "Reagan, you okay? You're awfully quiet."

"I'm fine," I said, staring out the window. We arrived home and got the boys to bed. I told Steve I had a headache, so I was going to go to bed too. I went into our bedroom and sat next to my hope chest. I pulled out my mom's white shirt and held it to me. Trying to breathe her scent into my soul, I began to weep into the fabric. I cried and cried and cried some more. Finally, I reached for my phone and looked at the text from Matthew.

Reagan, I wanted to let you know that my dad passed away tonight at 9:07. He was surrounded by me and my mom. He went very peacefully, which I am thankful for. It feels strange to be so profoundly sad and so utterly relieved at the same time. Take care, Matthew

He's gone. He's really gone for good this time. I looked into the hope chest and pulled out the white envelope. I wanted to see his writing . . . his words to me. I pulled out the letter, and something else fell in my lap. I picked it up. It was a photo of Jonathan. He was standing on a golf course about to take a swing, and he had the hugest smile on his face. He looked so happy. I stared at his eyes, and he seemed to stare right back at me.

"I'll carry the memories for both of us now," I told him. I turned off the lights and crawled into bed with my mom's shirt and hoped that one or the other would visit me tonight.

Chapter 27

A few weeks later, I was sitting on our patio on a Saturday morning, enjoying a rare moment to myself. Steve's parents had gotten four tickets to the zoo through some raffle and offered to take the boys. I was drinking some coffee and finally started reading the book I had taken off my mom's shelf months ago, the same book her wish list had fallen out of. I looked over at the bucket of garden tools and knew I should really do some yard work, but it was just so nice to sit and relax.

I saw my phone light up, and a text from Matthew popped up. I picked up my phone quickly and read his message. *Reagan, I just wanted to let you know that I am back in Colorado. My mom is settled into a new routine and seems to be doing okay. Okay as she can be. I can't ever thank you enough for coming out to Florida. You are truly a very special person, and although I know it's not possible, I wish we could stay in contact. Take care of yourself and all the best to you. Matthew.*

I heard Steve coming outside, so I quickly put my phone away.

"Why don't we go to lunch? We can go someplace that we actually want to go to for a change," he said.

"Sure. I'm going to head inside to take a shower first," I let him know.

"Okay. Oh, can you text my mom and just let her know we'll be gone for a little bit? I'm not sure what time they are bringing the boys back," Steve said.

"Yep," I said and headed inside to the shower, texting his mom along the way. I set the phone on the sink and started the water. As soon as it was nice and steamy, I climbed in and let the hot water pour down on me. After a few minutes, I heard Steve open the door.

"Reagan, I think I'm going to shave in the other bathroom. Is my razor in there?"

"No, I put it in the cabinet," I replied. I heard him rummaging around. After a few moments, I called out, "Do you see it?" There was no response. I peeked my head out of the curtain, but he was already gone. *Must have found it.* I finished showering, got dressed, and let Trixie out before going to eat. I watched her sniff around the backyard, and I heard Steve slide the patio door open. He stepped out and sat at the table. I walked over by him to ask which restaurant we should go to, and he stared at me. In a tone I had never heard in all the years I'd known him, he said, "Reagan, who is Matthew Carlson?"

The world stopped. It literally stopped.

"Where did you hear that name?" I said slowly, reminding myself to keep breathing.

He held up my phone, and I saw the text. *Reagan, I forgot to tell you if you ever do need to reach me, it would be probably be best to call me at work.* Next to that was a series of numbers.

"You're reading my texts?" I asked him. *Yeah, that's it. Deflect it to him. That's fair.*

"Your phone lit up when I was looking for my razor. I assumed it was my mom texting us when she was going to bring the boys home. Who is he, Reagan?" he asked, looking into my eyes.

"It's not what you think," I said.

"Yeah? What do I think?"

I sat down next to him. I took a deep breath and said, "Matthew Carlson is the son of the man I had an affair with twenty years ago."

"Why is he contacting you?" he asked.

"Steve, what I'm about to tell you is not going to be easy, but please, please just hear me out," and with that I began the story. I told him about the first phone call, the cancer, and the decision to go to Florida. I told him about my time there, leaving out some of the details that he wouldn't understand. I told him that Jonathan was gone.

"So, you never went to Illinois? You flew to fucking Florida?" He stared at me with disbelief.

"I did."

"You lied to me . . . about all of it. How could you do that to me . . . to the boys?"

"I had to for me. You wouldn't have understood," I told him.

"I understand you just took years of marriage, trust, and faith and threw it all away on a weekend getaway."

"Do you really think that's what it was like? I needed closure, Steve."

"Fuck closure," he threw back at me and stood up, indicating he was going to leave.

I grabbed his arm and began to sob. "You don't know. You don't know what this has been like for me losing my mom. Every fucking thing reminds me of her and what I have lost. I think of the last meal I ate with her when I cook one of her recipes. I picture her kneeling in front of her rose bushes when I walk in my dad's yard. I can't get the image out of my mind of her holding out her arms to me to give me a final hug. I think of the defeated look on her face when she looked at my dad for the last time in that hospice bed. I can't even put up my Halloween decorations without picturing her hospice room we so pathetically tried to decorate. I will never, ever talk to her or see her again the rest of my damn life. I will never be able to close the door on this and not think about this again. Because with death, you never really get closure. There's always a conversation you wish you had but didn't or an event that just reminds you they will never see anything of your life or your children's lives again. And I don't know, maybe I thought by going out there I could get the closure with Jonathan that I never really had with my mom. There is no way I am going to be able to make you understand this, so you're just going to have to accept it." I began to sob quietly into my hands.

"How will I ever trust you again?" Steve said quietly.

"I don't know," I said, shaking my head and looking up at him. He walked back into the house, and I sat in the backyard for a long time. Finally, I got up, and I slowly moved over to the bucket of garden tools. I pulled one tool out, walked over to the area of rose bushes, and stared at the vibrant colors.

"So, how do you do this?" I asked out loud and began to prune the roses.

Jill M. Bagurdes is a wife, mom to two sons, and a teacher.

Her favorite things are her cairn terrier Trixie, Mexican food, a glass of Moscato, the color teal, and decorating her house with things she finds at craft fairs.

She loves spending time with her family, especially when there is a board game or good movie and popcorn involved.

She cherishes her friendships…especially those with T. L., S.B. and C.K., who have always stood by her side.

She has always had a passion for reading and spent many hours with Judy Blume and The Baby-Sitters Club books in her younger days.

She does not like yard work but wishes she knew how to prune roses.

Her quest to find rose petals continues.

This is her first novel. She hopes you connect with her story.

www.ingramcontent.com/pod-product-compliance
Lightning Source LLC
Chambersburg PA
CBHW022151240626
47153CB00007B/2607